WINTER CHILLS

VOL. 2

LAYNE ADAMSSON   A. Q. HART

S. J. LOMAS   DAN MACDONALD

8N PUBLISHING

Cover concept and design by Sarah Perry.

Print ISBN: 979-8-9879774-1-5

Ebook ISBN: 979-8-9879774-0-8

❀ Created with Vellum

Contents

To my mother, who raised a daughter who refuses to suffer in silence.
To those of us who are more powerful and resilient than we ever thought possible, we will survive to better days.
-A.Q. Hart

SHE GIVES ME LIGHT

A.Q. HART

Why does the moon stay tethered to the earth? The moon, powerful enough to move oceans, to blot the sun from the sky, to affect the very biology and psychology of humankind, why does she stay? Is she trapped? Does the moon throw herself to the apex of each end of an ellipse, only to be brought close again by Earth's gravity? A body drifting by, caught in an orbit she could not escape. But one day, the earth will weaken, and the moon will peacefully drift away. Or maybe she won't go so peacefully. Maybe she will crash into the Earth. With all the stars she once knew so painfully far away, with nothing to lose, she will deal Earth a punishing blow before departing.

The beam of the cold moon shone down on me through the window. The daydream she inspired dissolved into my reality as the shadow of a lazy snowflake crossed my vision.

For most, the holidays are a hectic time at best and can be a dark time at worst.

John and I were firmly in the hectic category this holiday, hectic but happy. His parents had come down from Vermont to celebrate with us. His sister, brother-in-law, and their kids had flown from L.A. It had been non-stop entertaining for the entire week. At some points I would have forgotten my own name if John wasn't right there with a sweet, "Annabel, honey are you alright?"

John had just left with his sister and her family to the airport to catch their red-eye, all concerned about leaving me here alone, but there just wasn't room in the car for all of us. And considering the accident, we all agreed it seemed best for me not to be driving right now. It just wasn't proper to have house guests take a taxi to the airport. I could still see the worry in the corners of his eyes that didn't match his wide smile as John closed the front door at 8:45 pm.

As I sat on the couch, surrounded by the whirlwind of mess that three kids under the age of ten hath wrought upon our living room, I reflected on how little attention John's sister, Judith, gets from her husband. How lucky I was that John and I found each other. We were such a good match, and he was a good man. I could never forget that.

John had insisted that I just sit and rest while he was out for the two or three hours it would take to get to the airport and back, but looking at the aftermath of the extended visit, I wanted to get a head start on cleaning so John might have a tidy house to return to.

I started by tackling the piles of wrapping paper and coloring book pages littering the floor. One all the way under the couch caught my eye. I remembered John had accidentally crumpled it up and made our little niece Madeline cry. I pacified her by eating some salt water taffy with her from the container her grandparents had brought. I uncrumpled the drawing and smoothed it against my skirt. It was a drawing of John and I, but my feet were replaced with a fish tail. I had told Maddie I loved the beach so much and hadn't been back since my accident. Staring at the picture, I could almost smell the salt of the ocean in my nose. I went to the kitchen to make some electrolyte drink. John had said it was important to replace my electrolytes after the accident. I stuck the rumpled paper to the fridge with a magnet before getting out the water pitcher. The wax in the crayons caught the moonlight from the window in some places. Drawing me locked eyes with human me as I sipped my beverage. The brightly colored sport drink was much more thirst quenching than the tap water, but it didn't really hit the spot.

Having emptied my glass I felt better and decided to tackle the mess of wrapping paper, packaging, and whatever else was left around downstairs.

I shuttled back and forth to the kitchen with full bags of trash. A squeak in the floorboards under the area rug by the table that had bothered me all week, nagged me like a bone stuck in my teeth.

Once all the garbage bags were ferried to the back door, I returned to the area rug. I isolated the exact area where the squeak was worst to just beside the dining table and moved the chairs out of the way. Rolling back the rug, I saw the culprit immediately. A nail was sticking up out of one of the floorboards. We were so lucky none of the little ones had caught their foot on it.

I'm sure John would be able to fix it, but I didn't want to bother him with it, and I knew he would be so tired when he got back from his drive. Although I didn't usually get into the tools, I didn't see why not. Judith had talked about all her woodturning classes. Why couldn't I just use a little hammer and surprise John with my small repair? Maybe he wouldn't need to know, male pride and all.

I went to the entryway closet and got the small tool bag off the shelf. Placing it by the offending board, I settled down next to it and fished carefully past a small saw and a pair of pliers before I found my target, the hammer. When I pulled it out, the handle was coated in a sticky oil-slick substance. I looked back in the bag and saw the substance in the saw teeth and on the pliers. What a mess. I thought for a moment about the best way to remove any staining it might cause. Baking soda and a spot of dish soap in warm water probably.

I went to the kitchen and returned, this time with some rubber gloves to protect me from whatever this gunk might be. Now I was ready to remedy the squeaky floorboard. The nail was completely bent over. It would have to be replaced. I had found a small package of nails in the tool bag without the oily residue, thankfully. I wedged the claw of the hammer under the bent nail head and levered the handle away from the nail. The board unexpectedly came away with the hammer.

Well, not the entire board, just part of it. There was a cut in the board, the edges unstained and without any fastenings. The other nail that should have been holding it down was broken off entirely. Now that I got a closer look at the area, there was a bit of sawdust stuck to the underside of the rug, and the source of the squeak was much more obvious. The space between the floors under the missing floorboard was dark and vacuous. We were so lucky no one lost a foot into the floorboards. What kind of house would they think I kept with the floor in such disarray just under the dining room rug? This was maybe beyond what I dared to fix after all. I took another look at the part of the board that had come up. I had missed it before in my focus on the nail, but the piece of board had a dark mark. Almost like something was burned into it. A pattern of some sort—

I was staring at the ceiling.

It was the ceiling above the couch in the living room. This was how I usually came to after one of my episodes, with John by my side. The holiday had taken more out of me than I realized. I must be getting worse. It happened once right before the holidays and again during, which was extremely upsetting for the family. I had been in the middle of teaching little

Maddie to play Chutes and Ladders on that very rug and then next thing we all knew I was on the ground. It scared Maddie almost half to death.

I sat up slowly to see how I felt. No dizziness or nausea like there was sometimes when I had to be laid up in bed for a day. Thankfully it seemed mild. It would stress John out to know I had another fainting spell. I knew he wouldn't want me in the tools when he specifically asked me to rest. I should at least put everything back so I can casually mention the squeak to him when he gets home. He usually cleaned up my mess when I got like this, and then when I came to he was there to check on me. Looking back towards the table, everything was put back as if nothing had happened. Maybe he had gotten home while I was indisposed.

"John," I called out. Only the silence of the house answered me.

I looked at the clock on the mantle above the fireplace, it was 9:22. If it had taken me about thirty minutes to dispose of the paper, and look at the floor, I had been out for approximately five minutes.

I tried very hard to remember putting the tools away, putting the gloves away, placing the wood piece back, unrolling the rug, putting the dining set back, walking to the couch, and lying down. I couldn't remember doing any of it.

I walked to the entryway hallway and confirmed John was not in the downstairs bathroom. Then I went up the stairs, trusting my own constitution less and less every step. He was not in our bedroom, the guest bathroom, nor any of the three guest bedrooms. I was alone in the house.

Was it possible I imagined the whole thing? Did I clear the wrapping paper away? Was there a squeak at all? Was the floorboard broken? What about that marking on the wood? Was it also a figment of my illness?

I slowly made my way downstairs, feeling fine physically,

but rattled emotionally with so many concerning questions swirling around my head. Could my illness be progressing when I otherwise felt completely fine? Was it all in my head? Could I trust my own thoughts and observations? Was I much worse than we thought?

I reached the bottom of the stairs. There were two possibilities laid before me. Either I had imagined the entire thing, and I could not be trusted to be on my own at all, or I had just lost some time before I laid down. Neither was particularly desirable, but I had to know which it was, then I could decide which was worse.

The entryway closet where the tool bag resided caught my eye. That could be the first test, the existence of the sticky oil slick substance on the hammer. I approached the closet, opened the door, took down the tool bag from the top shelf, and sank down to the floor with the bag. Crouched over the bag, I eased open the zipper slowly. The entryway light spilled into the bag, finally falling on the hammer handle, shimmering with the blue-green-purple substance. I wrapped my hand around the hammer as if to make sure it was real. It felt as I had remembered, sticky over the smooth finish of the wood handle. Relieved, I let out a breath I hadn't realized I was holding. So I hadn't imagined the tools. What about the cleaning I had done?

Leaving the tools on the floor I walked down the hallway parallel to the stairs and entered the kitchen. The bags were stacked neatly by the back door. Ripping one open revealed it was stuffed with wrapping paper like I had remembered. That was another confirmation. Had I imagined the floorboard?

Leaving the kitchen, I entered the dining room through the arched passway next to the hallway door frame. I eyed the spot in the rug motif where I had isolated the squeak before. As I stepped on the spot, it squeaked comfortably. My favor for which outcome I preferred was revealing itself in my actions. Emboldened, I stacked the chairs beside the table to make room to roll up the rug with surety in my movements. My toes brushed the edge of the carpet as I prepared myself mentally for both outcomes. I slowly rolled the carpet back. The bent nail came into view. What would it mean if I saw the mark on the wood again? What would it mean if I didn't? A minor delusion. A spot of dream logic in an otherwise confirmed set of circumstances. Maybe I could live with that.

I tried to visualize what I had seen before and it was hazy and undefined in my memory. I slowly rolled the rug a bit further and saw the bottom of the mark. As soon as I saw the bottom half I could remember what it looked like. I rolled the rug up further to get a better look—

I was staring at the ceiling.

Again.

Why? How could I be looking at the ceiling once again? I bolted upright, the spark of adrenaline in my extremities. I looked at the clock immediately. It was 9:32. If it had taken 5 minutes to check the house for John, check the tools, and get the courage to check the floor again. Then maybe I took a couple minutes to move the dining room furniture. That left just a couple minutes unaccounted for. I looked from the clock to the dining room. It was reset again.

I walked straight from the couch, through the doorway into the entryway and turned towards the closet. The tool bag was open on the floor before the open closet door. Crouching down next to the tools, I reached down and upended the bag. The discolored handle of the hammer glittered on the floor. When I pressed my finger to it, I felt the stickiness as I pulled away.

I practically jumped up and hurried down the hallway back to the kitchen. The black plastic bag ripped easily under my fingernails. Wrapping paper scraps exploded into the air and slowly rained down around me.

I took a moment to think through the dining room piece. I grabbed a pad of paper from a drawer and grabbed a pencil from the cup on the counter.

I stood before the dining room rug for what I hoped was the third time tonight and reviewed my previously laid out possibilities. Wholesale delusion seemed impossible at this point, considering I could confirm everything but the dining room, unless this was also not real. In which case there was nothing to be done. I had completely lost my hold on reality. The second possibility of lost time seemed basically proven. Taking note of the time would help confirm that. A third possibility was taking form in my mind. I could remember everything except what the mark looked like. It was a smudge in my memory, almost out of focus. The edges of the new hypothesis were formless below the surface of my consciousness. It felt too impossible to be real but simultaneously was starting to feel like the only possibility. I moved the chairs out of the way, one fell over the other in my haste.

In an attempt to remove the lost time from the equation, I looked at the clock, 9:34, and jotted it down. Kneeling down to the floor at the edge of the carpet, I threw my notes down next to me. The carpet rolled up quickly and familiarly under my hands until I could see the nail and stopped. Continuing very slowly, I rolled the carpet up until I could see just the bottom edge of the mark. I examined the sliver of the round edge. It looked as if it was burned into the wood. Too steady and deliberate to be an accident. Returning the carpet to definitively cover the mark again, I held it in place with one hand as I reached back and grabbed the notepad and pencil. Rolling the rug slowly with one hand, I revealed the bottom sliver of the mark again. With my other hand I positioned the notepad so it blocked my line of sight to the mark. I slowly pushed the rug away so the mark should have been fully exposed based on the size of the blurry smudge in my memory. Deliberately, I blinked.

I was still looking at the notepad.

Shifting my weight around carefully, I used my leg to hold the rug back. My hand left the rug and moved towards the mark. I reached my finger out to find it. It was hot to the touch and I pulled away quickly. Tentatively, I ran my finger across it and realized it was not burning, it was biting cold. I placed my finger on it again. I blinked.

I was still looking at the paper with my hand on the mark, hidden below it. The cold was slightly uncomfortable, but not painful. I pulled my finger away and examined it. It was slightly reddened from the pressure and friction. I rubbed my finger and thumb together. It felt unchanged.

I traced my finger around the edge to feel for some more information and construct its appearance in my mind. It was basically circular. I found a bisecting line that ran from top to bottom. I found another bisecting line that ran horizontally. I could feel there was something in the quadrants, but I could not feel the details clearly enough. I focused on the notepad I had been looking at vacantly.

Over the holiday John had insisted we all watch *North by Northwest*. Thornhill is able to track Eve to the auction by making a rubbing of the message pressed into the top sheet of the notepad through the missing paper above.

I put the pencil in my teeth and carefully isolated just the top sheet of the pad and placed it over the mark. Pencil retrieved from my teeth, I rubbed the side of the lead over the mark. Slowly the mark was revealed in its entirety. I blinked.

I was still staring at my loose pencil rubbing of the mark.

It was indeed a circle, with a vertical and horizontal bisecting line. The top left was blank. The top right had a line drawing of a simplistic eye. The bottom left had a swirl that went counter clockwise from the center out. The bottom right had a broken horizontal line.

I lifted the paper carefully and stuck my finger underneath to rub the blank space. There were no details my untrained touch could identify. I rubbed a little harder to no avail. I pulled my hand back away and replaced the paper. My finger had the faintest sheen of blue on it. My attention returned to the rubbing as if looking at the symbols would reveal to me how the sight of this combination of marks could bring my sickness on. I had to share this with John. This seemed important, some kind of key to my illness. Maybe I wasn't sick at all. This was something else. He wouldn't have to worry. I brought my focus back to the paper, and the right edge of the rubbing caught my attention. It looked like I had caught the previous message in the pad of paper like the detective from the movie. The revealed part looked like, "DO."

I grabbed the pencil again and rubbed the lead around the letters. I didn't understand what it meant but my stomach dropped and a shiver ran down my spine.

DON'T

TRUST

HIM

I released the rug by moving my leg, and it rolled back over the mark. I stared at the ominous message for another couple moments. I flipped the notepad closed and looked at the cover. It was a girly one, with different sized pink and purple hearts covering it. Not the type of thing John would probably use. I flipped back to the message and thought about who could have written it. I took the pencil and rewrote the message myself.

The handwriting matched.

I wrote the message.

I had no recollection of writing this. Who was it referring to? Why would I write that? Who did I write it to?

I passed my hand over the revealed message and felt the impressions of more writing to uncover at the bottom edge. I used the pencil again.

Flour

I ran to the kitchen, placed the pad down, and pulled the flour container from the cupboard. I pulled off the lid and grabbed a slotted spoon from the drawer. I swirled the spoon back and forth through the flour, pulling up a spoonful of flour a few times. I couldn't feel any resistance that didn't just feel like flour through a slotted spoon.

I stuck my hand into the jar and felt nothing but flour between my fingers. In desperation I overturned the flour onto the kitchen island granite top. Ensuring the container was empty. I examined the outside. The transparent plastic revealed no secrets. I used both hands to push the flour around. The container wasn't set on the counter entirely and in my concentration I knocked it to the floor. A puff of residual flour billowed into the air. There was nothing but flour. I rubbed handfuls between my fingers. I tasted what coated the tip of one of my fingers and tasted nothing but uncooked flour.

Turning towards the flour coated rubbing, I stared at the message again.

Flour

I looked up towards the ceiling, wracking my brain for what it could mean. A yellow box caught my eye.

Flour

The vintage ceramic dry good containers on top of the pantry, yellow with hand painted labels.

Salt, Sugar, and *Flour*.

I scrambled on top of the counter adjacent to the pantry and grabbed the container. The lid slid off and shattered on the floor. Still standing on the counter, I tipped the jar towards my face and looked inside.

There was a piece of paper.

With the jar tucked under my arm I got down from the counter. I placed the jar on the counter and pulled the paper out.

It was a folded white piece of paper ripped from a notebook.

I slipped my finger between the folds. Opening the second fold and revealing the message was like lifting a weight off my shoulders. I couldn't read what was written fast enough.

Before you do anything else, you must be alone.

If you are not alone, replace this note and restore it to its hiding place. Revisit this when you are alone. DO NOT TELL JOHN.

When you are alone, recreate the note in the pad of paper by rewriting the message with a pen and burn the top piece of paper. Replace the notebook in the drawer.

To stay strong and sharp, add 3 cups of salt to your electrolyte drink mix.

If you fail to follow these steps, your life will be in danger, Annabel.

You are not crazy, and you are not sick. There was no accident.

Where is your family?

Who were you before you met John?

Who are you really, Annabel?

You know it does not add up. If you must, replace the note and return when you can't accept it anymore.

Each paragraph was written with different ink types and colors. As if written at different times.

Maybe I was worse than I thought. Maybe I was delusional. Maybe I had paranoid episodes, and there was a sick part of me that did not trust John. I would have to show him when he got back. I did all the cooking. He rarely came into the kitchen, except to take out the trash through the back door. He would never find this without me. He didn't know how bad it was.

I ran my fingers over the letters, undeniably written in my hand by a me I did not know or remember, but I felt inexplicably drawn to.

I turned the note over in my hands and on the back were two words written large in the center of the page in my handwriting.

Red Sky

I knew exactly where the next step in this scavenger hunt would lead me.

What would be there when I got there?

I left the kitchen, headed down the hallway towards the front of the house, and turned up the stairs. I could feel the flour stuck to the bottoms of my feet as I climbed to the bedroom.

I sat at my vanity and couldn't help but look at myself in the giant mirror for a moment. I looked harried and tired. My hair was a mess. My lipstick faded. There were circles under my eyes, flour stuck to my cheek.

I turned my eyes towards my makeup. There in my tray of everyday wear items was one of my black plastic tubes of lipstick. I picked it up and found the shade name on the bottom.

Red Sky

I looked around the tube. The case was shiny and cool. The surface was unmarred. I opened the tube and extended the tube of lipstick. It was a cool deep red. When I looked closer, the edge was misshapen. As if something had shaved off some of the side. With the tube turned towards the light, I looked into it. There was something lining the inside of the lid. I grabbed my tweezers from the vanity and pulled it out. It was a piece of paper. Lipstick smudged the ends of my fingers and the vanity as I unrolled and unfolded it .

Salt makes you stronger.

Moon blessed salt gives you strength he cannot wipe away. It lies with the other skies.

To make more, set a jar of salt out overnight during the full moon.

Use it wisely. We will need it.

Goosebumps prickled across my skin.

Moon blessed salt and gathered strength.

The other me believed in the occult. My curiosity was winning over logic though. Where was the salt? Other skies...

I opened the drawer in my vanity where I kept my backup makeup and things I used less often. After a couple swipes through the sealed packages, I found a container I didn't recognize. It was a vintage glass Avon jar filled with coarse ground salt. I opened it. The salt smell was overpowering. I was so thirsty. I hungered but not for anything I should eat. I was overwhelmed. The coarse chunks were pinched between my fingers and straight to my tongue without a second thought. The sensation of the salt dissolving in my mouth was exquisite. I closed my eyes in bliss. In my mind's eye I could see the salt moving through my blood, fortifying my body, sharpening my mind.

I opened my eyes and saw myself in the vanity mirror again. My eyes were more alert. My cheeks had a little color. The circles under my eyes faded. I regained some control and shut the jar. After a moment the salt smell faded and I felt more myself, but the vitality I saw in the mirror seemed to stick.

I was losing it. I needed to find out as much as possible and show John so we could figure out what happened to me when I created this unhinged scavenger hunt.

Was there another step? I turned the lipstick note over.

On the back was a single word.

Uneven

Uneven was a very vague clue. Maybe it was indicative of how wild my fantasy had become, that other me believed I would be able to follow a scavenger hunt with such an unhelpful clue.

Uneven

I could not deny however, that there was one visual hovering in my mind at the word. I would go and see, and there would be nothing, and I could know that this was truly madness. It had no rhyme or reason and did not actually lead anywhere. It was fool's gold. It was alchemy. It was impossible.

I returned back downstairs and into the living room, in front of the unused fireplace. There was something wrong with the chimney and we never used it, or really needed it. Crouched down, I brought my eye level to a brick that had never lined up correctly and always caught my eye when I sat in this room.

The back of the chimney wall was stained black with soot from the previous tenants, presumably. We actually kept cast iron logs in the wood holder, to keep the fireplace from looking empty and sad. In the fake wood and along the floor was ash. Soft ash that turned to dust against my fingertips. The directions of the first note had instructed me to recreate the invisible note in the notepad and burn the top page. I attempted to estimate how many pages would create this much ash. How many times had I done this? How many times had I set about gathering evidence of my alter ego's crimes, only to get swept up in the madness?

When I could tear myself away from my harried thoughts the mislaid brick was all I could see.

I reached out to trace the edge of it. The masonry was cool against my fingertips, black soot smudged with ash. At the corner, the brick wobbled slightly. I pressed it again. It was loose. I reached out with both of my manicured, but lipstick-stained, hands and dug my fingertips into the tiniest lip of the brick that was sticking out. My fingers strained and lost purchase. I tried again, focusing on my fingernails. The texture of the brick scraping against my nails set my teeth on edge. The brick finally started to loosen and I could use the pads of my fingers to grip. The brick came free of the wall. The recess into the wall was a black hole. I climbed into the fireplace, over, atop, and around the metal logs. Scraping my shins and thighs to get a better look. I saw nothing in the hole. I poked my sore fingers around the recess and found nothing but the rough edges of brick and mortar. I examined my hand. There was a bit of that blue-purple sheen around a couple of my fingernails. A closer examination did not reveal any more. Where had it come from?

I climbed out of the fireplace and looked at the brick. There was no more of that blue substance on the brick in my hands. In the back, there was a slender groove, smaller in diameter than a pencil, with something white wedged into it. I pried the white object free. It was a dense cylinder of rolled paper.

The brick discarded, I found the edge of the paper and unrolled it. It was another note.

To understand what has happened to us, you must believe something unbelievable.

Magic is real.

It has been used to hurt us, and it can be used to fix what is wrong with us.

The magic follows this format. 3 symbols and one source of power, in an unbroken circle, created and joined with intention.

Draw this to see for yourself.

In the empty space add some ash for power.

A flame for outcome.

A hand for direction.

A blue jay for color.

Remember we have sacrificed so much for the knowledge. Protect it with your life.

There was a circle reminiscent of the rubbing in the floorboard. I blinked.

I was still looking at the symbol in the note.

It wasn't exactly the same though. The top left was blank, where the ash would go presumably. The top right had a flame; the bottom right a hand; the bottom left a bird, the blue jay if the note was to be believed.

I rubbed my finger in the soot from the fireplace and sat back to draw the symbol on the floor.

A circle the size of a dinner plate centered between my legs. I created my horizontal and vertical lines to break it into four segments. Then set to work on the symbols. I didn't consider myself much of an artist, but the images I thought would be a poor approximation at best were eerily similar to the note's sample. I reached in and pinched some ash between my fingers.

I leaned over the symbol to smudge the ash into the empty section. As soon as I had swiped once I was startled at the intense heat on my chest.

In the center of the symbol was a blue flame. There was a blue fire. There was a blue fire on the hardwood floor. Fire! I scrambled back until the couch was at my back. I kicked myself around and turned to smother the flame with a throw blanket. When I turned back towards the fire, blanket in hand, it was gone. There was a scorch mark in the center of the symbol. The symbols in the burned part of the floor were etched into the hardwood as though I had carved them with a knife. Cautiously I reached towards the black mark. It was still very hot, but not injuriously so. What had caused the flame to go out? A smudge in the bottom right corner caught my eye. I checked the bottoms of my feet. On my right foot was a smudge of black soot joining the flour. I had broken the circle and the flame had gone out.

The state of the living room floor settled over me. John was not going to believe this, that magic was real. Hopefully that discovery would take the sting out of the ruined hardwood. Maybe there was a spell for that as well.

Looking at the fire spell, if that was the right word, I had trouble wrapping my head around it. I couldn't help but think about the symbol I had found on the floorboard. Had I "cast" that spell too? Who is the "we" and "us" referred to in the notes?

Where was the note? A moment of panic gripped my chest. Had it been burned with the magical fire? As I hopped up on my knees I heard a crinkling and saw it slightly crumpled between my knee and the floor. I picked it up with a relieved breath and held it to my chest. I couldn't stand the thought of not seeing this to the end. I couldn't call this all a delusion if magic was real, but I was also afraid of how I had used magic without remembering. Had I cast a spell on John? Had I cast a spell on myself? Was it why I was sick?

I couldn't remember feeling sick after creating the fire. If anything I felt... stronger. More steady. Less feeble. Less sick.

How far did this rabbit hole go? And what would be waiting for me at the end?

I un-crumpled the note clutched to my chest and flipped it over to the backside, hoping for another clue. I was not disappointed.

Hair

I had a secret I had never shared with John, or a single other soul. He had gifted me a locket for my birthday. I couldn't help but think of the old Victorian custom and the locket's namesake tradition to keep a small lock of your lover's hair in the locket. In the night while he slept I took my tiny tailor scissors and snipped the smallest lock of his hair from the back of his head. I tied it with a piece of thread and hid it behind the picture he gave me.

There wasn't another person in the universe that knew this. I took the necklace off from around my neck and popped it open to examine the inside. I expected the small bulge behind the picture on the right of us holding hands, but not the warp of John's picture on the left.

I used my fingernail, sore from the brick extraction, to lever out the picture. There was blue around the edge of the picture, this mystery stain I kept finding everywhere. In the locket, wedged behind the picture's tiny frame was a square of white. I used my nail to lever that out as well. It was a very compact note. I unfolded the note with unsteady hands, shaken by its proximity the entire time. Right below my literal nose was evidence of this double life I had been living, my secrets and false reality.

Annabel, do you see it yet? Do you see what he has done to us?

We know he has the spell book. We do not know what he still intends to do with it. We have lost so much progress to its use, but we could not alter or steal it without alerting him.

His workshop in the basement is where the grimoire is kept. But you must follow these steps to access it covertly...

I took the paper to the basement door. I never had any occasion to go down there. It was his personal space, just as the kitchen was mine, but admittedly with less privacy.

I don't know why John would have such precautions. I believe I would know if my husband was casting spells in the basement. Maybe I was the one leaving sigils around and leaving traps on doors I didn't need to enter. I consulted the note again.

Remove the hair from the door frame without breaking it.

My eyes traced the edge of the door for the supposed trap, and there in the top corner, almost out of reach was one of John's blonde hairs taped to either side of the doorframe.

I untaped one side delicately with the edge of my finger-nail and at the last second the fine strand of hair snapped. My fingers were filthy and there was now ash, soot, flour, and the blue-purple residue on the sticky side of the tape. I had been careless. I could probably wash my hands and re-tape the hair with fresh—

No. It was already happening. I was getting swept up in the notes. I was slipping away. I didn't need to re-tape anything. I was gathering as much as possible to show John, and we could figure this out together. I hoped.

The deep breath I took steadied me. I could do this. I tried the door and it rattled against the lock.

Take a pencil with an eraser.

Use the left sigil to unlock the door.

I took my pencil and drew the sigil on the door above the door handle. A circle and four quadrants. A keyhole, a key, an open door, and the smudge of ash, soot, and the oil slick mystery substance on my fingers in the empty spot. The lock shot open so fast it sounded like something cracked. When I turned the handle for the door it did not return to level after. It was broken.

I opened the door. John could help me replace the door handle later. I stepped onto the top step, and used the pull chain on the stairway light. The illumination fell down the stairs and disappeared into darkness. It smelled musty and stale.

When you enter the stairway, look at the poster just inside the door frame. Lift the bottom corner without the tack and break the circle of the sigil there with the eraser.

There was a singular poster on the left wall. An old adver-tisement for Ivory Soap. There was no thumb tack in the bottom corner. I lifted the corner slowly. Two sigils looked back at me, side by side, like some perverse mirror.

I examined the sigil, in the upper left a brown rusty

smudge, then around clockwise a symbolic bell, a stepped line like stairs, and a foot. I used the eraser on the back of the pencil to break a line in the circle.

My pencil in one fist and the note in the other, I descended.

I stepped out of the pool of light from the stairs into the dark, reaching above me with the pencil hand for a pull chain or light switch. I dropped the pencil and it went sliding across the floor under something I couldn't quite make out. There was a noise behind me. I froze. My pulse drummed in my ears, pressing against the silence. I heard it again, a wet noise. I held my breath. This time I could tell it was a dripping noise. I turned around slowly, my hand still reached out for balance in the dark until it brushed a box. I felt along its face and switched the light on. I braced myself to face the potential horror. There was nothing but the open expanse of the basement. The noise happened again. It was the work sink against a support pillar in the center of the basement. The faucet was dripping. I had never been down here. It would make sense that I would have at some point, but I had no memory of this space, how it was laid out, or what was down here. The shape of the room held no familiarity. There were peg boards with tools lining most of the walls. Workbenches below most of them. Some had fixtures like vices attached. Some had saws atop them, or embedded in them. The tools on the peg boards ranged from saws and pliers, to sets of vials.

I approached a set of vials close to me. "Mustard," "Mugwort," "Mandragora." This was not my handwriting.

I couldn't think about what that meant for my plan or hypothesis.

The grimoire is in the lowest drawer of the filing cabinet.
On your way out, replace everything as it was.
Replace the line in the sigil.
Replace the hair on the door.

Use the right sigil to re-lock the door.

We cannot take the grimoire out of the basement unless it is certain we can break free. We think he will know.

I identified the filing cabinet in the corner. It was old and rusty where it met the floor.

I squatted down on my heels and opened the bottom drawer. A thick book covered with an inky black leather sat flat and squarely in the center of the drawer. The air around me suddenly felt dry and dusty, in contrast to the wet and musty smell just a moment ago.

I reached in with a shaky hand and grabbed the book. Its size was surprising. It felt as heavy as a book two or three times its size would be.

I sat back on the dusty floor and rested the book in my lap. I could feel the edges distinctly on my thighs.

The cover lifted easily, like something beyond the force of my hand opened the book. The first few pages turned immediately after the cover to the title page.

The Briar Hags Grimoire, 1302

A few more pages turned seemingly on their own.

A Spell For Reducing Power

The pages flipping now could not be confused with gravity or momentum from the cover. The pages flipped quickly, as if a stiff gust was blowing across them, but the air was stale, and it didn't explain the pauses that came as suddenly as they went after I read the title of the page.

A Spell For Partial Binding

The pages came faster now.

Summoning A Sea Spirit

As if the book knew I had accepted the impossibility of natural causes for the page changes, a huge chunk of pages flipped over. The cover pressing into my thighs with the impact and the dull noise echoing in the basement.

Complete Bindings

The book did not move again after I read the title.

I have not found a way to bind a creature completely. It may not be possible. It also seems irresponsible to document even if I was successful, knowing the nature of man. I will not document or pursue it any further.

The corner of a piece of paper was sticking out, bright white, against the yellowing of the pages in the ancient book. I flipped to the pages the loose paper sat between and pulled it out to reveal the grimoire page underneath.

Forgetting Spell

The target of the spell will forget what they have done for 80 breaths and undo what they have done before returning to a spot chosen with intention. Many afflictions of this spell cause one's memory to become faulty. When inscribed into the skin of the target, specific memories can be repressed with intention. Created to relieve one afflicted with a traumatic past. If they are exposed to many details of the spell or their past, the spell will be undone.

The page I had pulled out had a hand written title in ball-point pen ink.

Complete Binding by John Grimm

There was something breaking inside of me that I did not know was there until it started to crack.

My hand shook against the book. I unclenched the crumpled note in my fist and flattened it out gently with trembling hands. It was the back side of the note.

It had much more than one word.

We have yet to find the item he uses to bind us, or the substance of power for the spell, or where the sigil is that imprisons us. We are so much more than this existence he has subjected us to and without the missing components we will not be able to return to what we are meant to be.

The sound of something falling onto the paper broke my train of thought. There was a wet spot that destroyed the letters. The ink swirled within it. My fingertips found my cheeks wet. A tear had run down my face, off the tip of my nose, onto the paper.

I felt sick. I felt panicked.

I had not cast the spells.

I had not been wrong. Magic was real, and it had been cast on me. I did not remember my family, my past, who I was, because my memory had been taken from me. Again, and again, and again.

My skin felt constricting, like my hand was in a glove that was too tight. My insides strained to get out. To take their true form. I couldn't breathe.

John had done this.

I had written the notes. The "we" of these notes was me reaching across a divide of time and interference to free us, all of us he had erased.

John had trapped us.

My complete breakdown was interrupted by a distant but piercing noise. After another stilled moment it happened again. It was my telephone. I grabbed everything in my lap and ran up the stairs. I tripped over the top step onto the landing in the front entryway, the book flew open to the back cover. A red powdery smoke spilled out emitting a high pitched shriek.

I covered my ears with both hands against the auditory assault.

The sound suddenly stopped. When I pulled my hands away my palms were slick with blue-purple.

I took a few moments to catch my breath. My head was pulsing against my skull. My fingers still felt too tight against what was inside of me.

The ringing started again. I clambered up and stumbled into the living room. The sound led me to the couch, where my phone was. I did the only thing I knew how to do with it, which was answer.

"Hello?" My voice was hoarse and unfamiliar to me.

"Annabel? Are you ok, darling? The alarm—" Johns voice was equally unfamiliar to me. The warmth was sickly sweet, and sounded disingenuous to my ringing ears.

"What?"

"The alarm... company called. They said the alarm had gone off. I'm nearly home. Are you alright?"

We didn't have an alarm.

"Is everything alright?" He repeated. Nothing was alright. I was at a loss for words. How much had gotten by me before? How many times had these flimsy excuses worked? How many times had he turned around my confusion from his violation of my mind back on me?

"Annabel. Are you still there? Are you well, sweet?"

"I was just..." I looked at the scorch mark in front of the fireplace. "...resting. Like you suggested, John."

"I'll be there in five minutes. Don't worry. I'll take care of everything." He hung up.

I looked around at the state of the downstairs. I couldn't put it back. I had failed us. I could not pretend everything was normal the way it was. I had amassed all this evidence to show John what I had been up to. Everything we had lost to time and tampering then worked so hard to regain would all be lost.

There was a giant burn mark in the floor in front of the fireplace. The brick missing from the fireplace had left an imprint where I dropped it. The ashes, soot, and blue-purple spread around by hands, and footprints, and drawing. The chairs in the dining room were knocked over. One leg was actually broken. In the kitchen I could see flour coating the floor, shredded paper and broken porcelain were scattered all over.

What could I do?

I could not put it back. There was no hope to go back.

There was no hope, unless I could end it, unless I could unbind us. I could only move forward.

My heart was pounding in my chest. Five minutes. I looked at the clock. It was 11:47. I had five minutes. Forward. Forward meant breaking the binding. I reexamined the back of the note I found still in my clenched hand. I accidentally ripped the corner free in my tensed fingers as I opened it back up.

The item he uses to bind us...
The substance of power for the spell...
The sigil that imprisons us...

These are the three things I was missing to free myself. *The sigil that imprisons us.* I thought about the locket. What if John had used something like that. I yanked my wedding ring off my finger and poured over every edge and facet. It was a plain band with a simple solitaire raised stone for an engagement ring. There wasn't any place to hide anything. The stone was secure. There was no sigil or engraving on either of the bands.

There were so many places to look in the house. The components I needed could be anywhere. I looked towards the kitchen again, and remembered the floorboards. The mystery that started it all. I just had to not look at the sigil.

I ran to the rug, my dusty feet sliding against the hardwood and falling onto my hands. I threw the rug out of the way, some of the chairs jostling around again with the force.

I closed my eyes and felt around for the nail. When the metal met my hand I pulled it and threw it in the direction of the kitchen, out of sight.

I looked down into the hole in the floorboards.

There was something I could just barely make out in the darkness. I reached my hand into the unknown space. Everything I could fit in my hand was pulled up onto the floor. My hand touched a cylinder of some sort. I pulled it back out to examine it. It was a small glass vial with what looked like some of that same oil slick substance, some red residue on the walls of the glass, and a large pointed blue-purple scale. As big as the bowl of a tablespoon. The top was sealed with wax that dripped down the sides, a sigil pressed into the top. I sat the vial aside and reached back into the hole and pulled out a stack of old magazines tied with twine, the pages weathered yellow with age. Good Housekeeping, Family Circle, and Ladies Home Journal among them. There was a tag tied with the twine with a sigil on it. I realized I could recite the articles corresponding to the cover stories. John had put this in my head somehow. I had no recollection of reading these magazines. I didn't have time to think about this. I pulled the twine off, ripping the tag in half in the process. My mind was more my own than it had been for as long as I could remember. There was no useless knowledge on how to please my husband, or award winning braised beef recipes, or how to keep my hair style for seven days after my appointment. There was room to think. I flung the magazines across the room. Several pages coming loose and fluttering in the air. I reached my hand back into the hole finding nothing but the wood surrounding the space.

I revisited the vial with the strange scale, holding it in my hand again. It felt oddly warm in my palm. Could this be one of the components I needed? I heard a whooshing in my ears, like the wind across the ocean, louder and louder until I could hear nothing else.

Then there was the sound of glass shattering and silence. My hand came back into focus. I had crushed the glass in my hand. The mixture of blood and the blue-purple substance was dripping from my hand. I sucked in a breath as I peeled back my fingers slowly. Chunks of glass fell to the floor. I braced for a wave of pain, but it never came. It didn't really hurt. The scale sat in the center of my palm coated in the oil slick liquid, and trails of blood swirled around. There was barely any blood, but I could see the glass sticking into the flesh of my palm and fingers. There was a lot of the mystery substance. I pulled some of the glass out. The oily liquid just kept coming, dripping down my arm and through my fingers. It was oozing from my cuts.

Was this coming from inside me?

This was my blood. I was not human. I was a summoned and bound creature. Of course my blood was not red.

The pieces started to fall into place. The substance of power was my blood. The shimmering blue-purple liquid on all the sigils was my blood. It was how John was controlling me. He was harvesting my blood and wiping my memory. I was not human, but he was the monster.

It was at this moment that I heard the jingle of keys in the front door lock.

I froze for a split second. I hadn't found the sigil binding me. I could not escape. John would know and take all the knowledge away from me. He would know every hiding place we had cultivated. He would know we knew.

I ran to the couch and laid down in the position I had woken up in countless times before. I had always assumed John had laid me down like this after finding me passed out somewhere. It was actually a spell to control me, not a doting husband, but a jailer.

The door creaked open.

"Annabel."

The door shut. A hesitant step.

"Annabel?"

Footfalls approached the doorway to the living room. I shut my eyes.

"Annabel! Oh darling. You really overdid it, didn't you? All this resetting isn't good for you. But I'll fix it. I'll make it so we don't have to use those anymore." His hand caressed my cheek. I pressed the scale and glass shards into my hand for the courage to keep from shuddering.

Would he free me? Did he realize his mistake? Was he not quite the monster I had assumed he was?

He left my side and walked back towards the door. I heard him rummaging through the tools by the closet.

He returned to my side. I was focusing on keeping my breath even. I hoped this was something he expected. I was relieved and disgusted that he acted as though a trashed house and my catatonic state was behavior that he had seen before.

"You know I had an epiphany while I was on the drive home. I had been so afraid to leave you alone. Something like this always happens when I do. The lesser binding spell called for blood. But blood changes over time. Blood loses its power. It dries and coagulates. It isn't static. What if we could use something of yours that was more... permanent. More unchanging. That's when I had a lightbulb moment." His hand brushed across my lips.

"Bone. We'll use bone to do the full binding."

My deliberately slowed pulse started to race again. Was he going to cut me open? Take one of my bones? Break something? Could I stop him?

His hands started to part my lips.

"So we'll just take a tooth. No one will notice a molar missing, now will they?"

I let my jaw go slack. I needed another moment to think how to stop this, how to break free. His hand reached into my mouth, deep to my back molars. I fought a shudder as his wedding ring clinked against my teeth, and I realized where I had seen a sigil before tonight.

John's wedding ring. He wore my binding in plain sight, cast right into his signet style ring. My eyes flew open. John had one hand in my mouth and the other wrapped around the handle of the pliers, poised to enter my mouth. If I could just get the ring off.

John froze.

I angled his fingers a little deeper into my mouth and bit down as hard as I could. I thought about the moon blessed salt I had eaten and the intention another me had set to be strong and sure. As John's screams filled my ears, and John's blood filled my mouth, I thought about all the versions of me he had murdered. The time I had lost to his hubris and folly. As he stabbed my face and cheek with the pliers in an attempt to free his hand I thought of how free I would be when this skin wasn't holding me back. I thought of when I could return to the sea. He wrenched his hand back and forth, jerking my head around.

A memory returned unbidden of a time we were in a similar position. In the ocean, on the beach, when he summoned me, before stealing one of my scales, and placing it in a glass vial. My blood mixing with his, binding me to him.

John's hand came away from my face, and I was afraid I had failed. He scrambled backwards on his back toward the fireplace. The loud thump of the grimoire tumbling from his lap onto the floor punctuated a small moment of silence before John looked at his hand and started to scream. Blood gushed from his hand, streamed down his arm, and soaked into his shirt. It streaked across the floor in his wake. He screamed and screamed. "You monster. You bit my fucking fingers off. Annabel! You bitch. You cunt. Fuck you! I will fucking destroy you. I will get another."

I removed his two fingers from my mouth and examined them in my hand. I pulled the ring off the finger and wiped some of his blood away. There was the sigil. The symbol of my binding. How brazen. How monstrous. It was cast into the metal. I didn't know how to break it.

John continued to scream at me, how he would undo me.

How he would destroy me. But he couldn't catch his breath. He kept looking at his mangled hand. Tears streamed down his face.

I saw the burned floor next to John. The scorch marks were filled with John's blood in a very satisfying way.

I dipped my hand into his blood on the floor and started to reinforce the fire sigil I had written earlier onto the floor with his blood. I would see how he liked the turnabout.

John realized what I was doing and crawled towards my glyph on his knees and elbows, shaky like a newborn fawn, slipping and unsteady. His hand reached out to break the circle but he just added more of his blood. He couldn't break the circle of his blood with his blood soaked hands. I looked around for anything to stop him. I reached for the brick from the fireplace. By the time he thought to go for me instead, it was too late. I pulled my arm back and up and hit him in the face with it as hard as I could. The impact broke his glasses into his eyes and knocked him backward. His screaming began anew, but this time with less coherent thoughts, more curses to my name.

I completed the glyph and the blue fire erupted in the floorboards for the second time tonight. I threw the ring into it.

John seemed to realize what dire circumstances he was in. He blindly, desperately reached towards the fire. When he found it he hesitated before plunging his hand into the fire. I scrambled up and jumped on him, using both my hands to hold him there so he could not remove the ring. His screams lost any meaning. It was like music to my ears. He held the ring in the fire, but I held him.

The confines of this body tied me to this meaningless exis-tence. To John's mistake. To 1950s housewife magazines. The restraints of the binding spell slipped away as the ring softened and the sigil lost shape in John's broiling hand. He screamed and convulsed under me, but I was strong.

My freedom washed over me, my power restored, and it was like taking a first breath. It was like feeling the wind on my skin after breaking the surface of the water. Laughter erupted from me as I rolled off of him. It is a wonder that the tiny spell had ever held me. John screamed and I laughed.

He attempted to strike me with his unburnt but mangled hand. I brought the back of my hand across the face of the screaming, burning, bleeding man, and he crumpled face first into the ground. I sat up and dug my nails into his skin as I picked him up by the scruff of the neck like a bad pup. He tried to push against me, tried to pull away. I flipped him over, held him down against the ground, and straddled him. With one hand I restrained him by the neck as I dug my hand into his chest with the other. I pulled out his still beating heart and marveled at the feat of magic that is human life, and how it is wasted. What was left of John gurgled and sputtered before becoming limp under me.

Climbing off of John, I tossed his wasted heart into the blue flame. It will blacken and harden to reflect his true nature. May it be more useful as ash than it was in flesh.

I considered the grimoire on the floor. It existed for many a century, and would have gone on many a century more, had it not been tainted with his abuse, by his malicious blood. I rendered it to kindling, sad for its waste, and fed it to the fire.

Lit by the flare of the blue flame catching on flesh and parchment, I stared in awe at my body as it slowly started to return to its natural form. I stretched and sighed. I was covered in my blood and his blood. My clothes shredded against the scales poking through my skin. I walked to the entry hallway, threw open the door, and looked back into the house, my shadow in the doorway dark against the stark moonlight. I would not miss this place. I felt no need to bid it goodbye. I turned and walked down the steps. Snow fell slowly and peace-fully against my face. The moon shone down on me. Instinc-tively I turned towards the sea and walked leisurely into the dead of night.

Let them wonder what happened to demure little Annabel. Let them share whispered worries. Let them follow my bloody footprints to the sea.

ACKNOWLEDGMENTS

Thank you to my husband, Matt, for always supporting my schemes and adventures. I likely wouldn't have had the guts to start writing again if it wasn't for Miko, the most inspiring best friend I could have ever dreamed of. Thank you to Sarah for giving me a shot. To the members of the Danger Eye Tea Society, thanks for contributing to my survival over the past few years. Last but not least, I give thanks to you, dear reader, for letting my story rent a little slice of your brain. I hope you enjoy your new tenant.

ABOUT THE AUTHOR

A.Q. Hart, aka Annaka Hart (she/they), is a horror and romance author who also narrates and produces audiobooks. They are from Las Vegas, Nevada but have never gambled. Her goal as an artist is to create more magic in the world, but she does not believe in astrology. Their pastimes include: gardening, destroying the patriarchy, and roller skating. She does not like talking about herself in the third person, snow, or ketchup. They live in Michigan with their spouse and colony of freshwater aquarium shrimp.

Learn more at www.AnnakaHart.com and follow everywhere @AnnakaHart.

TIPPING POINTS
LAYNE ADAMSSON

A cold-nosed starfish peeks from beneath a carpet of snow. Its rainbow arms sweep the world clean and for a giggled moment, the universe knows nothing but crystalline joy.

Fern wipes the frozen memory away with the nighttime ice filigree decorating her tiny kitchen window. There's no time to indulge in reminiscing. The fire's gone cold. The musk oxen are stirring. Movement is both survival and solace.

Tipping coffee dregs onto the frosted skeletons of her garden, she sighs at the thought of eight months without fresh fruit and vegetables. She'll get by, she always does, but she's already longing for the pungent scent of tomato vines; never a good way to start autumn. Shuffling a damp path through the drusy edged birch leaves, she makes her way out to the paddock where her shaggy little herd clusters, patiently observing as dawn spreads its marmalade glaze across the eastern horizon.

"Morning Gladys," she murmurs, offering her open palm to a steaming investigation from the matriarch's muzzle. These quiet behemoths always make her smile. The big bull, Q, shedding immense quantities of qiviut each spring, always manages to vex and delight Fern. Gladys' younger sisters Iris, Daisy, Violet, and Pansy are gentle, watchful, and protective of their surviving yearlings: Cedar, Maple and Willow. For now she's still calling Gladys' calf "baby." A real name will come eventually. Family takes time.

Feed and hay down, hens out, eggs collected, Fern takes in a breath of musty leaf litter freed by the warming sun. "First snow'll be here soon, I s'pose," she pronounces to the unblinking sky. A shiver of birch branches and a soft snort from the paddock are the only replies.

Fern carefully washes the breakfast dishes to conserve each precious drop of tank water that must be hauled back out after use. She pauses to watch a chittering junco at the feeder outside her kitchen window. They were Rory's favorite. She scrubs the pan harder, trying to cleanse the recollection from her mind, but as she moves to drying, she can't help but finger the frayed edges of her lonely life. What would it be like to hold onto limitless love? How can people form bonds stronger than water? What allows some to expand and contract through the seasons, contorting into something elegant, buoyant, while others simply break and sink?

When the loneliness threatens to fossilize her, she boils the kettle and rummages through the stack of newspapers delivered last week. Catching up on the news ought to be sufficient distraction for a few hours at least. The headlines are certainly unsettling if not diverting. Coastal communities in a flurry over the startling rates of erosion and thinning sea ice. Emaciated polar bears wandering progressively further south. Predictions of worsening forest fires. She sips her tea picking through threads of fear and rhetoric looking for data.

Carding and spinning all the wool she's collected from the musk oxen, the woods, and the neighboring herd over summer will take months; plenty of time to meditate on solitude in a rapidly changing world. Most people would approach these tasks systematically, clean it all, card it all, spin it all, but Fern knows monotony kills. Instead, she selects one bundle at a time, attending it from "mess to finesse," treating herself to the delight of knitting it up into functional works of art before moving onto the next batch. She knows it's not efficient, but who needs to worry about efficiency when there's so little else to do through the long, dark winter?

****

Eight times warmer than sheep wool, qiviut is the finest fiber in nature–softer than cashmere. The first time Fern cast on a row of this enchantment, she was hooked. Maybe its effects were heightened by the flood of oxytocin after she and Rory first met at the trading post. Maybe she would have fallen in love with anything he touched. Maybe the world would still be spinning on its axis if he hadn't spun her off hers.

He was trying to convince the owner to let him sell raw fibers on commission because he wasn't interested in "all the fiddly work." Fern was instantly captivated by his relaxed but confident cadence. She sidled up to the men under the pretense of interest in the product. When it was clear the owner wasn't keen on stocking tangled heaps of raw, unwashed wool, she proposed to be the middle-woman. Rory considered her worn Carhartt overalls and muscled arms with a long slow gaze as a gap-toothed grin spread across his face. Extending a hand of partnership, he explained how to find his homestead the next day to "talk turkey."

Fern hadn't a clue what she was doing as she bumped along the rutted, rocky excuse for a dirt road twisting between drunken black spruce off of the main road, frost-heaved into a lurching roller coaster. She'd never carded or spun wool, and she'd never fallen in love, yet here she was suddenly jumping head first into both. She hadn't even considered what she was offering with her business proposition. Somehow, it made perfect sense in the moment. Her PhD research was stalled due to funding gaps, she hated waiting tables almost as much as the customers hated her, and that work would dry up when the first snows froze the tourist dollars anyway. She liked knitting and figured it couldn't be *that* hard to spin. But all the logic came after the reason.

He'd shown her the bags of qiviut he'd collected in the wild over the years during his summers documenting ecological markers; spoke rapturously on his solivagant expeditions. He introduced her to the small herd of musk oxen he'd coaxed into his river valley and expounded on his commercial ambitions. Explained their feeding, breeding and molting patterns with the patience and passion of the brilliant professor he could have become. Finally, he sent her off with a test batch. If she could successfully spin it into soft gold, he'd give her 10 kilos to transform over winter.

It was an agonizing month of research and experimentation as Fern desperately tried to get the process right. Her eagerness to see Rory again pushed her and made every failure doubly frustrating. Eventually she had a skein worthy of the trading post's investment.

That was the first time she had to wait out his indefinite absence. The only means of contact was to leave a message at the trading post, where he would eventually leave one in reply. She only had so many excuses to stop in, but that was the trouble with casting your lot on a man at loose ends, you never knew when it would all unravel.

****

At the carding table, Fern thinks about signs she's seen, echoing the newspapers' alarm bells: the growing asynchronicity between flora and fauna, infrastructure damage on the roads and in town, stressed trees, the crumbling river banks. She swiftly pushes the final chip from her mind; it's too heavy to hold. She started the research 20 years earlier, before they'd known enough to be sure what was happening, what could happen, what would happen, but early enough to change course. Her mind wanders as her fingers pick bits from the tangled mess before her, like random data points trying to represent a vast complex web of interrelated variables.

She wonders if she could have made a difference. Where would she be if she'd persisted instead of being pulled into Rory's world. Woven into the fabric of this severe landscape, all her broken threads knitted then unraveled again by the life they pieced together. Could she have discovered some key evidence, something irrefutable to stop the climate denial before it started? Fern grits her teeth and focuses on combing. *It's madness to think like this.* Obstacles were already being thrown in the face of truth before her time. Funding cuts, paper rejections, derision, harassment, threats–she experienced it all. Rory was a welcome escape, not a scapegoat.

The rapid autumnal equinox slide always unbinds. Ghosts huddle in the lengthening shadows as the sun retreats to the southern rim of the sky. It's the slippery light of loss, the world going dark. Sometimes she can't breathe when the river's rushing song tangles in the wind, plucks her own lost screams from bare birch branches. This play of light refracting strands of life slipping through her fingers.

The rich velvet taste of salmon dinner for one transports her back to visiting Rory the second time. His palpable delight when she stepped out of her truck. The goosebumps he'd sent shivering up her spine. Her shriek of terror as Teekon, silent and lupine, materialised at his master's knee. The electricity of proximity and her impatience to tell him of her trials. The internal fireworks ignited by his indirect question, "stay for dinner..."

He'd served Copper River King with blueberry sauce, mashed Yukon Golds, fiddleheads and cherry tomatoes still warm from the sun. A royal feast. She'd asked where he found young fiddleheads so late in the season. His only answer was a wink and something about his "ways with ferns."

The memory still holds power over her after all these years. The tantalizing hope he would ask her to stay crushed in a winded blow when he'd ushered her out to her truck under the star-strewn sky. How her guts twisted on the dull blade of, "see you after breakup." A whole winter away.

He was as beguiling as the aurora. An elusive lone wolf. Thoughts of him danced through Fern's head with the phantasmic pulse of the green banner of sky above her. Unobtainable.

****

Fire, coffee, oxen, chickens, breakfast, spinning table. Fern's fall days have a cozy predictability preparing for the transition heralded by the first snow to stick. She doesn't bother with a calendar anymore, the angle of the sun is sufficient. She's taken aback when the northern lights dance across the sky before the first flurry. Unsettled by the expectant stretches of tundra she passes to pick up her final rations and newspapers for the year. Images of houses falling into the sea, the latest volcanic unrest closing Anchorage airspace spin through her mind as she worsts a batch of yarn. The world is changing whether she pays attention or not.

Control what you can; let go of what you can't. No more driving things with will and effort, pushing the future with dedication and brilliance. That was her way before her first harvest withered on the vine; before Ashton and his little sister-to-be. People always say children change you, but no one can possibly explain just how much.

****

That first winter without Rory was interminable. Fern set herself firm routines to complete sufficient skeins each month for rent and supplies. The radio, with its dependable schedule and commentary, kept her company as the dark months skittered around their sharp bend. It spurred meandering daydreams about Rory's bandy-legged lope, what he might say about the weather or news, how he could move to the music. How he might move with her.

Breakup couldn't come soon enough. Not just for Fern, but the whole of central Alaska straining against winter's icy grip on the Tanana. Grumbling patrons crowded the trading post speculating whether anyone would come close to winning this year's pool. Mocked by the tripod standing proud on the frozen river weeks later than it had for a decade, most predictions had long since come and gone.

The anxious anticipation of Rory's homecoming became unbearable. She fretted something would prevent his return. By late-May, as gravel-crusted piles of packed snow loomed on corners and studded tires were swapped out for the summer, the river ice broke free, and her hope rushed away with it.

Sloping into the post with her last bundle of worsted yarn, a twinkling of gray-blue eyes caught her completely off guard. Skeins scattered around her feet as she impulsively threw her arms around Rory's neck. Sensing him stiffen, she awkwardly disentangled herself and gathered the strewn yarn and scraps of her dignity from the floor. "You're back," she said flatly, not daring to look up.

"I am." He sidestepped embarrassment by inviting her over to discuss business. "I have a proposal for you."

***

The treadle's steady rhythm is a working meditation. Fern's mind traverses time spirals as the wheel transforms silken qiviut into a lifeline. Heart-quickening moments of endless summer days, back-breaking labors of love, crushing losses, renewed hope, then back around to the joy that brought her here.

Rory had much to show for his winter away. Electric with

nervous anticipation, Fern discovered a mountain of lumber, stone, hay bales, and wire stacked before the one-room cabin. Fluorescent flagging and spray paint highlighted trees and ground. "Need a summer job?" he called out, sliding down from a Bobcat loaded with earth. All she could do was nod and beam back at him.

Equally desperate not to wait tables and to spend every possible moment with this man, Fern didn't hesitate to accept his invitation. To transfigure this tangled patch of wilderness into a working farm side-by-side with someone who smiled at her with his whole self, who made her feel seen and strong, was an offering of grace. She moved out of her place to camp on the property. Together, they squeezed every joule from the unflagging daylight to clear and level space for extending the cabin, raise a hayloft, build a chicken coop, dig a garden, and fence off spaces for corralling musk oxen when necessary.

Manual labor was their courtship dance. Finding a groove, moving in harmony, anticipating the other's needs, actions. Every post hole dug, each nail driven, all the meals devoured in exhausted communion bound them closer. Words flowed sparingly at first, but spilled into torrents as camaraderie bloomed and evenings gave way to deepening blues. It was easier for two solitary, introspective people to speak in the umbra.

As they'd stood back to admire the finished cabin beneath the golden flutter of leaves, Rory asked Fern if she'd like to move in for the winter. Again, she threw her arms about him without thinking, but he reciprocated with equal fervor. "Take that as yes?" he laughed. She'd looked into his eyes and kissed him with the tidal force of a year's pent-up desire.

Living off-grid without running water was never easy, but Fern had never been happier. She experienced uninterrupted ease in Rory and Teekon's quiet steady company whether striding through the woods, driving into town, or dip-netting.

Every day brought new learning experiences; their mutual admiration mushroomed as she knitted while he read to her in the protracting evenings.

Each had a sublime surprise for the other on Christmas morning. Rory brought Fern breakfast and coffee in bed. Under the improvised cloche, she found french toast adorned with a sapphire ring. Wide-eyed and delighted, she beamed at him kneeling beside the bed. "It was my mother's..." She drew a deep breath and threw up over the beautiful service.

"I'm pregnant..."

***

Fern was never a Christmas person, but winter solstice always makes her pause for ritual and tradition. In the half-lit days before the sun makes its final bow, she carefully stacks fallen branches where she plans to dig new garden beds. The longest night bonfire will enkindle her spirits and warm the ground. Dragging downed wood into her clearing, she's struck by how unusually warm it is; it doesn't burn to inhale.

Fire symbolizes destruction and renewal. Every year she makes offerings to its hungry tongues: a tuft of gathered qiviut, salmon bones, a handful of moss, an eagle feather, three pairs of knitted baby booties, and a poem. This year she has written:

> *The weighted grains fell—between*
> *us heavy, expectant-edged, charged*
> *with need and electricity.*
> *Sands ticking slickened time—click*
> *a rattle of finite formed a solid stopped*
> *the curved edges of a universe.*
> *Folding back upon us—comfort or*
> *suffocation depending how we split*
> *our temporal Möbius strip.*

Prayers for safe returns, balance, and letting go. Every year, she expects grief to wane, its grip to slacken; every year she is shaken by its persistent intensity and the world's growing disquiet. The blended intoxicants of wood smoke, dancing flames, and a few nips of kirsch yields the most vivid night visions.

In the morning, she wakes cold and stiff, fingers itching to form what she has dreamt. Endless plans for hook and needle.

Spring curls its way into the valley with a shuffle of hooves returning from windswept ridgelines. Fern greets her musk oxen friends with alacrity and plentiful hay, checking carefully for injury or illness. Months worth of spinning and knitting are piled in neat boxes in her truck to exchange for the staples she's exhausted. At the trading post, Nenana Ice Classic winner announcements scrabble above the fold, but since the second winter without Rory, it makes Fern laugh bitterly. An annual gut kick. The brutal irony of a life bookended by the overpowering need to change the river's mind: once to make it flow, once to stop it in its tracks.

Yet she diligently notes when the waterway opens every year. Adds a single point to the graph she started plotting 30 years ago when complex systems percolated into her high school consciousness. She doesn't need to consult official databases or read the thinly veiled commentary buried beneath the contest fanfare to see the clear trend: the rivers are breaking up earlier.

Summer blazes to life. The tundra is unnervingly dry. She notes that the sponge-like active layer of berries and bracken perched upon permanently frozen ground is draining and sinking everywhere she wanders, plucking qiviut from bush and branch. The absence of mosquitoes is a welcome respite, but the permafrost is melting. Permafrost, nature's Pandora's box. The lid is off. Planet-kindling beasts released in unspeakable quantities. And the fires rage to life.

She retreats to her cabin. Comb. Clean. Card. Spin. Knit. Comb, clean, card, spin, knit. Combcleancardspinknit. The rhythm overcomes the dancer. The mantra moves the monk. She is a whirling dervish. The wool demands her hands. She loses the edges of days as the sun forgets to set; forgets when to feed the animals, when to feed herself. She starts to make a blanket and forgets to stop. Repetition and patterns soothe her, give her control, steady her breathing; seem to stabilize the world outside.

The fires sweep around the valley, but everywhere is smoke choked. She wraps wet fabric over her mouth, tries to tend her garden, and weeps when she follows the musk oxen down to the river. They are trying to breathe the cleanest air they can find and nearly drowning. Ashton swims through the dense air and she wails, haunted by the specter of a collapsing embankment. She runs toward him, outstretched arms exposing her face to the burning atmosphere. Yet again, she is out of breath and cannot reach him in time. She clutches her belly, drops to her knees, buries her face in the lichen and moss, and cries herself to sleep.

Gladys wakes her with a wet snuffling nuzzle. The other mothers loom protectively; Fern is one of them. She has no idea how long she's slept, but the smoke has thinned and she feels coherent. Hollow. The herd follows her back to the hay loft. Their insistence signals she's had a long slumber. A hunch corroborated by clutches of ungathered eggs.

Strict routines ground her. Clear objectives, subtasks, record keeping, and routine, routine, routine. Structure is the key to keeping your head when chaos and madness threaten. Fern visits the trading post, assesses the extent of fire damage from local gossip and papers. She buys a calendar and short-wave radio. Winces as the word "widow" follows her out the door.

Patterns emerge in the data: ocean temperatures rising, pH falling, glaciers and sea ice retreating, forest fires burning earli-er/longer/bigger. A north slope village is swallowed by the

Arctic Ocean. Unprecedented tropical cyclones batter the western reaches of the Pacific and Atlantic. She furiously knits global threats into background noise. She plots everything.

Bidding the herd farewell as they head to the windblown uplands for winter, she is gripped with an ominous sensation. Her foreboding intensifies as she lightly touches each one passing through the gate. This is the last place she saw Rory, shadowed by Teekon, when they were too bereaved to speak. When she needed too much closeness, and he needed the furthest reaches of space. She is overcome with an unshakable feeling she will never again see the only family she has left.

She cleans, she cards, she spins, she knits, she plots. Correlations she can't unsee. She stopped knitting during her first pregnancy and lost it. She stopped knitting before the river took Ashton, when she was too heavily burdened with his sister to run downstream, to jump, to save him. She couldn't lift her needles with the weight of so much loss dragging her under. And then Rory slipped away too. Lost to the wilderness he knew better than his heart, lost because his choosing not to return is agony, lost because his dying is unthinkable. Knitting is the only way to forestall calamity. Data do not lie.

Every night she falls asleep to the steady click of needles. Whatever else she must do each day to survive, her hands always return to the needles at night. Clean, card, spin, knit, plot; the world goes quiet. Winter grants her stasis.

Q doesn't return with the herd and Gladys spooks too easily. Fern can only speculate what might have befallen him. She loads her pack with a few days' food, knitting, and her shotgun. The forest beyond her valley is a graveyard of blackened skeletons haunting a ghostly gray landscape. She follows the herd's trail back to where they came from, looking for Q.

She is a scientist, but she's still human and nature's brutality still has the power to unhinge her. There is not much left of Q. Hungry wolves are incredibly efficient. She sinks to her knees in the bloody snow and screams curses to the impassive wind. Thankfully, the wolves are gone. Not because she's afraid of them, but because her rage is volcanic, ready to indiscriminately destroy everything in its path. It is the natural cycle of life, but it is a personal affront. Now she has nothing left of Rory.

In the long spring gloaming, she knits a pair of baby booties, ties one to each graceful curve of Q's horns. This is the shape of her grief. Every loss is different, but every loss echoes in the hollows of her heart and womb. She curls up next to Q's skull and dreams the dreams of wolves. Her teeth are sharp, her legs are fast; she works in unison with her pack, picks out the weakest, most defenseless, lunges. She wakes with the taste of blood in her mouth; her tongue aches.

The summer is besieged by visions. Rory floats in a strange fog. Wolves glide through the shadows. Ashton and his sister skitter up a tree. Fern trembles with the aspen leaves and knits. She forgets how to sleep, but there are no more climate calamities in the news cementing her resolve to control it all.

People warily eye her rare appearances at the trading post. Speaking in low tones and sidling away. Dimly aware of the apprehension, she projects her own anxiety about how to keep the world in check. She is oblivious to the schism yawning wider between reason and belief. Dissolves into the sugar, mixes into a bag of flour, condenses into canned goods. Phrases like "bereaved mother" only register as commentary on a dying planet.

Fern can scarcely bear to watch her oxen leave at autumn's frigid end. She feeds them extra hay and treats knowing it's folly to fight the unwavering current of their instincts. No new calves came after Baby and she weeps for never bestowing a proper name. Cedar has ascended to dominant bull, but the herd is unbalanced and insecure under his novice leadership.

Fern has to fight her own hands not to blockade their exit route.

Life is a blur of needles. Pine, spruce, metal, plastic, bamboo, ice. Needles up her spine, the cabin cold because she's forgotten to stir the fire. Pins and needles in her feet when she sits stone still except for flying fingers, working the wool for hours on end. Stabbing needles in her eyes after straining by lantern through endless Arctic winter nights.

Without Q, the qiviut haul is pounds lighter than usual. Her supply quickly dwindles working at this frantic pace. No crafting her usual assortment of high-demand items: scarves, gloves, toques, sweaters. Instead, an immense blanket spills over her lap, lumps across the floor, twists into a memory of Teekon's curled shape by the stove, Ashton's peaceful bump beside him. She weaves in the patterns of heady nights making love, her swelling belly and bosom, rising sea levels, hurricanes, and wolf jaws. A story unfolds at her feet.

When the last strands of qiviut wend their way from her skeins, she ravages her cupboards for means to save the world. Never-worn baby clothes unravel first, bleeding her heart dry. She moves quickly onto Rory's untouched drawers, all the beautiful things she made, her desiccated heart crumbles to dust and blows away. *Worse than grave robbery.* A thought lies still and unchallenged in her anechoic chamber, igniting a spark of inspiration.

Fortified with the edge of madness that slices through everything when honed by a certain idea, Fern bundles up, straps on her snowshoes, and pushes out into the razor sharp world. *Does a heart still break in the woods if there is no one there to hear it?* She scarcely registers the icy crust over the snow, which should signal the terrible tightrope she's treading. Freezing rain should not fall this time of year in the interior. She forges her way blindly up the river to the buried treasure she seeks, unearths Russian Orthodox hair, bones and teeth. With these macabre mementos, she continues to knit.

The March sun shouldn't be sufficient to melt snow from the trees, but soon branches are bare and icicles threaten from the eves. Still, she knits and pearls frantically, scavenges for more material to weave. Every scrap of fabric shredded to strips, she shivers in her last slivers and slips. Wires, fork tines, the furniture next. She raids chicken feathers, hay from the loft, prays to the moon that the oxen aren't lost.

She steals needles from the trees, grass from their roots, mycelium mats, fiddlehead shoots. The oxen are late, wolves howl on the zephyr, she spins it all in as the madness will let her. In come the wildflowers, willows like angora, she knits up the stars, the moon, the aurora. She winds in her loss, her sorrow, her pain, then blends in the meadows, the clouds, and the rain. Finally, she starts on her toes and her legs, turning the last page of her story. As she reels the weft in up over her face, at long last she again holds her Rory.

ACKNOWLEDGMENTS

This story was kicked up to the top shelf via ceaseless brain banter and stomach sharing with Deb Ewing. I can't thank her properly without profanities and weird animal phallus jokes, so I'll just have to leave it here.

About the Author

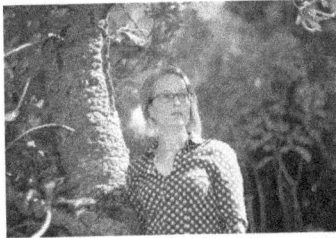

After decades of journalism, science writing, poetry and editorial work under other names, this is Layne Adamsson's debut fiction publication. Layne's work is a testament to her deep passion for physical sciences and literature, which she deftly weaves together. She is a tiny package of stone and soul, known to her writerly friends as "Blue", an interloper of Venn diagram intersections, a mad word connoisseur, and spawner of things that grow rapidly beyond her control. She is a collection of contradictions most commonly found tripping through the forest or hiding under a book when not spouting random fascinating facts.

Her poetry can be heard along the Ridge Walk, an immersive outdoor experience in the stunning Dandenong ranges of Victoria, Australia. Her letters to the trees are also incorporated into the Big Anxiety Festival and the Wind exhibition in the Climarte Gallery.

Her words are painted upon guitars, scrawled across unexpected surfaces in slime moulds, and occasionally beginning to appear in collections like this where others can actually read them (including the poetry anthologies *From One Line, Vol. 2*; and *Entangled*). Some day she hopes to put on her big-girl pants and get her novels and children's books published too. You can encourage such malarkey by yelling at her on Twitter @AspienBlue

ALL THAT GLITTERS

S.J. LOMAS

I never thought Lennox would convince me to come along to one of his paranormal investigations. Watching the occasional ghost show on TV together was one thing, but personally communing with spirits wasn't something I wanted to get involved with.

My parents had raised me to believe that ghosts aren't real, but that was often followed up with a "don't mess around with that stuff anyway."

It was completely different to Len's approach, which was to run headlong into anything that made people uncomfortable. In this case, I agreed with my upbringing, but I'd also known Len long enough that I couldn't let him down.

"Come on, Amy. You know I'm not going to let anything bad happen to you. Besides, it's a public event. The team's been here dozens of times. There's no bad energy there. You can do this."

I knew he was telling the truth. To be honest, I only half believed this stuff wasn't a bunch of theatrics just for entertainment. If Len was anything, dramatic was certainly it. But Len had told me a lot of stories since he joined the paranormal group. He was so earnest, and some of the experiences he shared gave me goosebumps. I couldn't help but wonder...what if?

He'd invited me along as a guest so many times, and I'd always had a valid reason not to go. Eventually, it became a joke between us. Amy the scaredy-cat who needs to wear adult diapers and carry a box of tissues to soak up her fear of ghosts.

It was comfortable to stay home. Besides, I wasn't going to get any bad energy attached to me if I just stayed away. So I stayed away.

Then Len asked Brad, the head of the group, if he could start leading public tours too. It took some training, but this was the first time Len would be in charge of a group. If ever there was a time to support my best friend and leave my comfort zone, this was it.

Another Michigan winter was in full swing. Piles of nasty gray snow lined the sides of the road, pock-marked from salt and road spray. Although it was only nine o'clock at night, the darkness made it feel like two in the morning. The forecast for the night was calm although we'd reached that sad, restless part of winter when everyone was just sick of being cold and in the dark.

Brad always ran his public hunts in October, when spooky season was in full form and ghosts and paranormal experiences were on everyone's minds. Len had insisted on doing his in early February and he'd explained his reasons to me months ago.

"First," he'd said, "Everyone expects October, but spirits are all year long. Second, it's colder, darker, and more depressing in February. People have abandoned their shiny New Year's resolutions and they're ready to sit in the truth. That's the perfect combination for opening up to the realm of the spirits." He'd waggled his eyebrow piercings at me for added emphasis. I, as usual, had shaken my head and smiled.

"Whatever you say, Captain. Just don't expect me to be there. It's too creepy."

Len had grinned. "You'll be there." There wasn't even a hint of doubt in his voice, even though I'd never gone. Hell, I hadn't so much as watched a scary movie with Len because I just found them too disturbing. Even the ones everyone thought were campy and stupid.

"I wouldn't be so sure."

Len had sat back and gazed down his nose at me.

"I am sure."

I'd crossed my arms, all mock-authority with him. "And what makes you so sure I'll finally break down and come this time?"

"Cuz you love me."

He was my best friend, of course I loved him. A sparkle of possibility lit in the back of my mind. I wanted to do it for Len, I really did, but I just didn't know if I could.

Fast forward five months and I was pulling into the parking lot of the historic theater where the ghost hunt was going to be. I guess what they say is true, love does conquer all, although I don't think fear of real or imaginary ghosts was on their mind. Whoever "they" are.

The marquee glowed yellowy bright in the desolate blackness of night. This was a unique type of darkness. Subtly oppressive, it seeped into your mind and stole your joy. It stirred a primal desire to hibernate, which could never be achieved. Even though the cold void of winter fought to steal my energy, it couldn't touch the excitement and dread growing with each footfall toward the entrance. For just a moment, I considered turning back to the safety of my car and telling Lennox something else had come up. At nine o'clock at night. On Saturday. Yeah. He'd know I was lying. Although he would laugh it off, I'd see that shade of disappointment draw over his eyes. He thought he hid stuff like that from me, but I always knew. It was why we'd become friends in the first place. Where everyone else saw a smart-mouthed weirdo talking about Edgar Allan Poe, slasher films, and ghosts, I saw a nice guy who desperately wanted everyone to think he was a badass. He'd been a new kid in eighth grade and I was drawn to him like the buttered side of bread to the floor. Most of the kids teased or ignored him altogether. I guess he appealed to my rule-following heart. Just enough bad boy to be thrilling, except that he wasn't bad at all. He wasn't negative or creepy, just open to other possibilities and confident enough to show it. I wanted to be like that. I still do.

I stomped the caked snow off my boots and opened the door to the theater. There was nothing visually unusual about it, other than the fact that it was apparently haunted. Whatever deep, dark, eerie atmosphere I was expecting was dispelled as I stepped inside. The first thing that hit me was the unmistakable popcorn and fountain drink smell. Salty and buttery goodness doesn't really scream "a ghost is going to steal your soul tonight!" However, it did make my mouth water.

The decor had nothing to do with potential ghostly encounters either. I guess if Lennox had booked it for October, there would be movie posters for horror flicks and monstrous creatures. Since it was February, the world had moved on from spooks and gore to matters of the heart. The lobby was decked out with framed posters of classic romance movies, like *Casablanca* and *When Harry Met Sally*, and strings of pink and red hearts dangled from the ceiling. There was even a display for a Valentine's double feature of 90s romcoms with a selection of heart shaped candies available for purchase.

The only indication of tonight's purpose was a long table toward the back draped in a black tablecloth. It had the Midnight Paranormal Group logo on it and a small crowd of people gathered around it. I figured I'd better head there first.

"Amy! You made it!"

Len had spotted me before I found him. He was heading over from the concession stand. He totally looked the part of "fearless ghost hunter." He sported spiky black hair with lime green tips, black eye liner, an eyebrow ring, a lip ring, black jeans, polished off with the black long sleeved t-shirt with the paranormal team's logo. He wasn't dressed the part of ghost hunter on a dark night. This was Len. He still loved to toy with people's expectations through his appearance. Odd couple that we were, I was wearing a camel overcoat with skinny jeans, boots, and a pink chenille sweater. My dirty blonde hair was down, to conserve warmth, and the ensemble was topped off with a wine colored knit hat my mom had made for me. Let's not forget my professorial tortoiseshell glasses. I would never admit it to Len, but I'd thought if I wore something light, maybe it would keep any unpleasant spirits away. If there were any at all.

I waved, not wanting to yell across the lobby to answer him. There were a fair amount of people milling around. It looked like it was going to be a good crowd.

He bounded across the space to wrap me up in a bear hug. "See? I knew you'd come."

His breath was warm on my ear, reminding me that I was still freezing from being outside.

"Let me get my coat off. I'm too cold to hug."

Len laughed. "Feels just right to me. Perfect ghost temperature."

Choosing to ignore that comment, I shrugged out of my coat and folded it over my arm.

"Did you get signed in yet?" Len asked.

"Nope. I just walked in."

He linked his arm with mine. "Then come on. Let's make it official!"

As we walked to the table, the young woman working it kept flicking her gaze to me and Len.

"Who's the check-in girl? She's trying to give me the once over even though she's busy."

Len glanced over.

"Really? You think she's sizing you up? That's Emlynne. She's really cool."

Emlynne was wearing her long brown hair in two braids, one draped in front of each shoulder. She also had the paranormal shirt on, but she'd paired it with a red skater skirt, fuzzy black tights, and knee high black boots.

Compared to her and Len, I looked like I'd be more at home with the romcom display than the ghost hunting crowd.

While we hovered at the end of the line, I took advantage of the quiet moment. I opened my purse before Len got swept away in the events of the night. "I brought you something."

Len's hazel eyes sparkled in genuine surprise for a moment before he went back into standard Len mode.

"You mean something other than this tremendous bravery of yours?"

I nodded and grabbed the little package I'd chosen to mark the occasion. It had gotten a little squished in my purse, but it still looked pretty nice.

"Whoa!" Len glanced from the tiny wrapped box in my hand to my face. "A proper gift?"

I handed the box to him.

"You've been wanting me to come do this with you for so long and tonight you're the head of the team. I thought that deserved a little something."

He carefully tore off the paper, exposing the shiny black box underneath. He looked at me quizzically.

"Open it," I urged. "I hope you like it."

He popped off the lid. It wasn't anything amazing, but his face lit up anyway.

"Number one ghost hunter," he read the inscription on the white enamel ghost pin I'd commissioned for him. "This is awesome! Thanks, Ames!"

He immediately pulled the pin out of the box and affixed it to his shirt.

"How do I look?"

He seriously puffed out his chest to show off the newly attached pin. A little ghost pin had just become his pride and joy. This was the sort of stuff people missed when they wrote him off. His less-traditional exterior was a great disguise for his buoyant, genuine, and geeky interior. It had always been obvious to me. I didn't know how most people overlooked it.

"You look like an official ghost hunter. Brad is going to be so jealous."

Lennox grinned. "A really hot ghost hunter or just an average one?"

"The hottest, of course."

Len and I were known for playful banter. It had always come naturally to us, to the chagrin of several ex-boyfriends and girlfriends we'd had over the years. Our dates came and went, but Len and I were forever.

"I'm glad you like the pin."

"I'm glad you came. Seriously, you're going to love this. I promise."

Although I trusted Len more than anyone, acknowledging the task at hand made my nerves jangle again.

I'm sure my smile was pretty feeble. All I could think of was melodramatic moaning ghosts like in *A Christmas Carol*. It wasn't reasonable, but the vision of a wailing green mist creature screeching through the theater seemed possible.

Len clasped my shoulder in a reassuring squeeze.

"Quit thinking the worst. It's not all *The Exorcist*, you know."

"I haven't even seen that. The trailer was bad enough."

Len chuckled. "I know that, but you get the gist. Think, something more normal, like the movie *Ghost*. Now that's a completely different vibe." He shot me a knowing look.

"Great," I deadpanned. "Now that's another disturbing set of circumstances I hadn't thought of."

"Don't worry. There aren't any pottery wheels here."

I didn't get a chance to answer because the people in front of us peeled away from the table and we stepped up to face Emlynne. She stiffened noticeably when Len wrapped an arm around my shoulders and hugged me tight. I may have an active imagination when it came to ghostly catastrophes, but I was definitely not imagining her reaction to me.

"Em, this is my best friend, Amy. Amy, this is Em. Her name is really convenient because she's our resident empath."

Len may have expected us to groan at his little joke, or humor him with a chuckle, but Em was appraising me with her deep brown eyes. There was a flicker of judgment there. Len and I were no strangers to judgmental looks when we went out together, but Emlynne's eyes weren't taking us both in. This was purely for me and she clearly didn't think I measured up.

For Len's sake, I held my hand out to Emlynne.

"I've heard so much about you." This wasn't a lie. "It's so nice to finally meet you."

She softened a bit when I said I'd heard about her, but she was still going to keep me at arm's length. Seemed pretty obvious to me that Emlynne had a thing for Len.

"Yeah, same." Emlynne took my hand and squeezed a tad harder than she needed to, but I supposed she was trying to mark her territory. Poor Emlynne. Len and I had been in each other's lives a long time. No jealous girlfriend or boyfriend was going to break up our friendship. If this was the path she thought she had to take, she'd be in for a rude awakening.

Totally oblivious to the secret showdown, Len rubbed his

hands together like an evil genius. "I'm going to take Amy around to meet the others and then it'll be time to start, don't you think?"

Emlynne peeled her gaze from me like she wanted me to know she'd be keeping tabs on me. She definitely had a flirty shimmer when she looked at Len. He'd mentioned her before, but not in a romantic type of way. No wonder she was mad. Definitely thought I was standing in her way.

"Sounds good." She smiled, all sweetness and light for Len, but he quickly turned to lead me to his team for the night: Travis, Chris, Grayson, and Barb. They spanned in age from the youngest, Grayson, twenty-one, to Barb, sixty-three. It was an eclectic group, which suited Len perfectly.

Introductions complete, there was nothing left to do but get started. Len moved to the front so he could welcome everyone. I took a deep breath as my heart started to pound. This was going to happen. I was really here to hunt ghosts with these people.

Just as Len started talking, two familiar men strolled in—Sterling and Carlisle, Len's older and younger brothers.

Len paused briefly in his introduction and nodded subtly at his brothers. I slipped from my spot in the crowd to intercept them.

"Hey!" Sterling's eyes shone with surprise recognition when he noticed me. "It's Ames! How'd he rope you into coming to this freakshow?"

Sterling couldn't have looked more out of place. He wore a long black overcoat, matching leather gloves, with a stylish wool scarf. His black slacks and leather dress shoes made it look like he'd come straight from the office...which shouldn't be the case at 9pm on a Saturday.

Carlisle was a mini-Sterling in training. Although he didn't seem to be wearing a suit, he did have on khakis and brown loafers, visible beneath his long gray overcoat. Their cheeks were red from the cold and I couldn't think of a single good reason they'd come out to see their brother.

"What are you doing here?" I aimed to be as neutral as possible. This was a big night for Len. I didn't want his brothers to spoil it. While I wouldn't say they all hated each other, they definitely had a dysfunctional relationship, mostly based on teasing Lennox.

"What?" Sterling carefully pulled off his gloves and tucked them into his coat pockets. "How could we miss the chance to see our dear brother do the only thing he's good at?"

Carlisle fought hard to contain the grin at his older brother's expense, but wasn't doing a very good job of it.

I crossed my arms over my chest and planted my feet squarely on the floor. "If you're going to act like that you can—"

"Geez, Sterling. You made Amy mad already. That's gotta be a record."

"Relax, Ames. Len's the one who makes scenes. Not us, remember? We just figured we'd come out and see what all this is about. Same as you, I'm sure. You've never struck me as the ghost hunter type. You're too smart for that."

I fixed them both with a warning look, as intimidating as I could muster, which probably wasn't even a little bit.

"It's good to see you, by the way. You're looking lovely as ever. Everything going well with work?"

The words could give the impression of being insincere, but I'd been privy to Len's complicated family dynamics for years. The brothers, including Len, were expert at belittling one another, but they weren't all bad. Despite their love of tormenting Len, they had always been very nice to me. Over time, they'd become like brothers to me too.

"Thanks. Yes, everything's going well, but you're making me miss Len's introduction. Get over here, be quiet, and behave."

Carlisle pretended to zip his lips and we joined the fringe of the group just as Len stopped talking. I couldn't suppress a frustrated sigh.

Len flashed a sympathetic glance at me. Missing his instruction was doing nothing to soothe my nerves.

"I've got these three in my group," Len gestured to me and his brothers. "So I can take seven more with me."

Emlynne and one of the other team members nodded and assembled their own ten person groups, so I'd apparently missed that we were splitting into three groups.

While people were moving around, Len came over to us.

"What are you guys doing here?" he aimed his question at Sterling. "This is serious. These people paid money for an experience—"

Sterling held up his hand for quiet.

"Chill, bro. We already got a scolding from your girlfriend here. We just wanted to see what it's all about."

"Yeah," Carlisle chimed in. "We're not going to mess up your freakshow."

The rest of our group was huddling in so they had to stop bickering and let Len get on with it.

"Watch it guys," Len warned his brothers under his breath before turning his attention back to our new group.

"Welcome everyone. As I said, I'm Lennox and I'll be your guide into the unknown tonight." He said it in a campy tone, which made it clear he was having a little fun with us.

Sterling and Carlisle rolled their eyes at each other but kept their mouths shut.

"Do we have any first timers with us tonight?"

Most of us, including me and Len's brothers, raised our hands. Len's face broke into a mischievous grin.

"Awesome! Well, thank you for coming out for your first ghost hunt. While I can't guarantee paranormal activity from our friends on the other side, I can guarantee that you're going to have a fantastic night."

"Does anyone at these things ever see a ghost?" Sterling asked.

I tensed beside him even though his tone was neutral rather than sarcastic.

Len turned to him as if Sterling was just an unknown member of the crowd, although, if anyone bothered to look they would see that all three of the brothers had the same hazel eyes and identical curves in their noses.

"Sometimes, yes," Len admitted. "I encourage everyone to stay alert and look around. You never know where something might manifest and often it's very subtle. Usually, we don't know a spirit was in the room until we play back audio or video recordings. It can be difficult to detect unaided, but some spirits have more energy than others and make their presence known."

A lady to my side linked her arm through her male companion's and squeezed. At least I wasn't the only nervous Nelly in the group.

"What if we do see something?" she asked.

"I'm glad you asked! If any of you see, hear, or feel anything unusual, please notify a member of our team. Depending on what you experience, we may be able to verify with our equipment right away. Don't be shy."

Carlisle looked skeptical.

"You've been here before, right? What experiences have happened right here in this theater?"

Even though Carlisle didn't seem entirely genuine, Len answered with enthusiasm.

"Most commonly, people see shadows moving across the wall, and since there's no light source once we get settled, that really stands out. Some people report feeling cold spots or like someone is playing with their hair when no one's around them. At this particular location, you might even hear whispering near your ear. It's pretty cool!"

All of what he said made the hairs on the back of my neck stand up. If it was anyone other than Len, I would have quietly excused myself to use the bathroom and not come back, but Len was so happy about his big night, I just couldn't do that to him.

"Okay!" Len clapped his hands together and made me jump. Sterling snickered at my foolishness, but no one else seemed to have noticed.

"As I said, we keep the lights off in the actual theaters where we'll be observing to limit interference. I'll be leading us in with a flashlight, but please watch your step. Take a seat wherever you want. Ready to go?"

The group mumbled a quiet assent. I don't know what my face looked like, but Len reached out and gave my hand a quick squeeze.

This little exchange wasn't missed by Carlisle, who nudged me with his shoulder.

"What's the matter, Ames? You're not scared of Len's ghost stories are you?"

Sterling tilted closer, eager to join in. "Don't worry. If a make-believe ghost tries to make-believe hurt you, I'll knock it back to the underworld faster than you can say, 'Sterling, save me!'"

It was definitely going to be a long night.

Len moved to the head of our group and led us off into the theater where we'd begin our journey.

Once I crossed from the well-lit lobby into the surprisingly intense darkness of the theater, things got real fast.

Len stood about halfway down the aisle and shone the weak beam of orange light onto the ground so we wouldn't run into the chairs.

As everyone filed in and found seats, the whispering of the participants stopped, including Sterling and Carlisle.

I'd never been in a theater without the brightness of a movie playing. Of course, there were still the red exit signs but their light only illuminated their own letters and not the surrounding area. It was like a nightlight in a stadium.

Thanks to Len's advice to look everywhere, I scanned the darkness wondering if I'd notice some sort of apparition. Not that I wanted to, but the atmosphere ripened my already fertile imagination.

My heart just about burst in my chest when I noticed the silhouette of a person in the projection room at the back of the theater. Then I realized it was just one of the other two groups who'd started up there instead of a theater. False alarm.

Now that we were nervously acclimating to the darkness, Len was truly in his element. It wasn't a word I'd normally use to describe him, but he scampered down the rest of the aisle with his flashlight and hopped up on the stage. Over the years, he'd perfected his moody, aloof, vibe that I so enjoyed about him. But being here gave him a whole new energy. He was actually bouncing on the balls of his feet with a big goofy grin while he made sure everyone was out of the aisle.

Out of familiarity, I suppose, Len's brothers stuck near me. I followed Len all the way down to the front and turned into a dark row of seats and they followed along. I stopped at what I figured was the mid-way point of the row and felt around to put down the seat. Carlisle took the seat right next to me. Sterling on his other side.

Once we were all sitting, Sterling leaned over his brother to whisper at me, "Does it feel cold in here?"

It was dark enough that I couldn't get a read on his facial expression. He might have been sincere, but it seemed more likely that he was just trying to freak me out. Nevermind that it was pretty chilly, but that was probably because it was dark and we were noticing things.

"Shhh," I said as quietly as I could and settled back into my chair, clasped the armrests, and fixed my eyes firmly on Len.

Once everyone was sitting, Len switched off his flashlight. It was so quiet, I swear we could have heard a pin drop onto carpeting.

With the slight comfort of a flashlight gone, my body became more attuned to the only sensory input around. It was definitely cold. I almost wished I hadn't taken my coat off. I crossed my arms over my chest to conserve warmth. Then I started to notice all the little sounds that are usually relegated to background noise—shuffling of shoes, creaking of the old theater seats, the breathing of the people around me.

Nothing had even started yet, but every nerve was at attention. My heart rate sped as if I was preparing to fight or flight.

"Listen to the sound of my voice."

I jumped, soothing quickly when I realized it was just Len. If I was this jumpy now, what would happen if we actually encountered something supernatural?

"I just like to say that once we're in the darkness because it tends to freak people out."

This elicited a few low chuckles from the group.

"For real though," Len continued, "the spirit world is only separated from ours by a thin veil. It's pretty easy to cross if you know how. Of course, it's just like dropping by to visit a living friend. Sometimes they're in the mood for company, sometimes they're not. So I can guarantee we'll reach through the veil tonight, but we'll have to see if anyone there is willing to play with us. That said, I've never had a silent night here, but it's my first time leading a group, I wouldn't put it past them to screw around with me."

There were some more chuckles, but the joke sent a shiver

down my spine instead. I knew Len's ghost hunting stories, but it hit me that spirits could possibly be in the room, surrounding us, at that very moment. The idea that they'd want to mess with Len, or maybe even me, didn't sit well.

I shoved my hands between my knees. My fingers were really cold. Even Carlisle next to me rubbed a hand over his upper arm as if trying to warm up.

Anxiety fluttered in my chest and the dark room gave me little else to focus on. Since no one could see me anyway, I closed my eyes and took a couple deep breaths. That seemed to do the trick.

When I opened my eyes again, Len was starting to explain what we'd be doing.

"The first thing we're going to do is use a spirit box. This is a tool we use to hear auditory phenomena in real time. In other words, we can talk and the spirits can answer."

There was that rapid heartbeat again. Conversing with a ghost didn't seem like it should be a terrifying prospect, but I couldn't shake the feeling that ghosts were swirling around the room, perhaps even in my personal space. It wasn't just that they were ghosts, but ghosts had been people. Who were these people? If they were dead, what did they know? Did they immediately have access to my life? It was unsettling in a way I hadn't anticipated.

Tucking my cold, clammy hands into my pockets, I tried to think of something else while Len got his spirit box contraption set up. Once he did, it did nothing to soothe my nerves. Not that I was expecting anything, but this was not it.

As it turned out, the spirit box quickly cycled through the white noise of radio stations. Len said it scanned seven stations per second. It was a maddening cacophony of static at higher and lower pitches. How were we supposed to talk to anything through all that noise?

In the darkness, I couldn't even use Len as a focal point to stay grounded. I'd assumed that he'd be smiling at me the whole time and then I wouldn't feel nervous. In lieu of Len's familiar face, I searched the darkness for one thing I could use to anchor myself in reality, the glowing red letters of the exit sign to the left of the stage. I concentrated on each letter and took long deep breaths. Eyes on something familiar, it was easier to keep myself from freaking out. Sterling and Carlisle would never let me live it down if I freaked out. Len would probably tease me too, but more than that, he'd be disappointed that I never shared this experience with him. That would be worse than any taunting Sterling and Carlisle could come up with. I had to stay calm, or at least fake it.

"We're going to go around the room and everyone can ask a question, and we'll see if we get any responses. Sometimes we can't understand it until we go through the recordings later, but other times it's clear immediately. I'll start so you get a feel for how it works, and then we'll just go around the room.

"My question is, if there are spirits in this room with us tonight, how many of you are there?"

The anticipation of everyone in the room was palpable. The air in the theater felt like it was being held as everyone strained their attention forward toward this oddly irritating box that Len had set up for us to listen to.

It took a few seconds, but then I heard it. The beginning was mumbly and hard to pick out, but then, clear as anything, a staticky voice said "eleven."

My heart stopped beating for a moment and even Carlisle went rigid next to me. The already cool air in the theater seemed to drop by at least five more degrees. Suddenly, it didn't seem like it could be a joke or a performance. All I could think about was eleven dead people floating around us at that very moment.

The next question came from a voice in the darkness.

"Do you need help to cross over?"

I wanted to keep my mind full of happy memories so I wouldn't pay attention to any more answers, but they kept being displaced by visions of Ebenezer's shrouded future ghost, plus a few swirling in the spaces between guests like ethereal ribbons.

It didn't help that a chilled blast of air blew across my face. Had someone turned the air conditioning on full blast to freak us out? I even turned to see if Carlisle had brought a personal fan to trick people with, but he was still, arms on his armrests.

Since I couldn't keep happy thoughts in my mind, I decided to try a mantra instead.

Ghosts aren't real. Ghosts aren't real.

Just because Len was my best friend and he believed this stuff, it didn't mean he was right. It was okay for me to stick with what my parents had taught me.

Even though I was thinking my mantra, it didn't manage to keep my ears from hearing the next question.

"Do you have a message for any of us?" Some man asked in a perfectly cocky voice. He was loud, not timid, and the whole thing filled me with dread.

Ghosts aren't real. Ghosts aren't real.

Just as I thought someone would toss out a new question, the temperature dropped sharply. I might as well have been standing out in the snow with no coat on. A particularly icy gust grazed my left cheek...the side no one was sitting on...and Len's spirit box made an electric sizzle sound. Then, clear as day, but tinny as an old phonograph, the message came: "Trade me."

The words came out of Len's device and slid into my ears like the poison used to kill Hamlet's father. It felt like ants streaming down my eustachian tubes, into my throat, and milling uncomfortably in my chest. They were taking hold in me and I didn't like it.

"Look here," called the voice. "I'm in the room. Do you see me?"

The words reverberated, like a cough, in my chest, compelling me to action.

I certainly didn't want to see an apparition, but I couldn't stop myself from looking.

My eyes were drawn to the glowing red exit sign. It was too high on the wall to be near an actual person, but dropping my gaze lower, I gasped.

It was like a shadow over darkness, but there was an unmistakable outline of a person and a mysterious flicker of gold that rose to eye level on the being, then back down to the waist. Slowly up it went, then back down. The pattern was mesmerizing.

"Amy?" Len's voice cut through the weirdness, but the things I was seeing remained. "What's going on?"

"There," I said, my voice wobbly. "Under the exit sign."

Seats groaned. People whispered.

"What are you seeing? Tell me." Len's voice held a vibration of excitement, but remained calm overall.

I described what I saw.

"Ah! You do see me!" The voice reverberated around my chest again, even though I heard it in my ears.

The shadow seemed to grow a little taller, and the motion of the gold sparkle stopped – hovering at the waist level.

"Hello." The voice sounded heavily processed, tinny with too much treble, but eager now too. "You really do see me, right? It's not just wishful thinking?"

"I," my voice came out in a rasp, so I tried again. "I do see you."

"Whoa! Is it talking to you?" Len was all excitement now.

"Yes," I said. "On your box thing. Doesn't everyone else hear it?"

The thought of being singled out by a ghost was even

worse than hearing it with all these people. This was exactly why I hadn't wanted to come.

"Don't worry about all of us," Len said. "This is your experience. What did you hear?"

The tittering of the crowd increased, but it was just unimportant background noise to me. I focused on talking with Len.

"Well, uh, it seems surprised that I can see it."

"Ok, yeah, that makes sense. It can take a lot of energy for a spirit to make itself known. Maybe this one is having an energy surge for some reason and it's not used to it. Maybe it was the message thing? It might have a connection to someone here. Ask about the message again."

I could feel Len near me as a buzz of excited energy. He was absolutely living for this bizarre experience. It wasn't what I'd imagined, but I was doing okay. Maybe there wasn't anything to be scared of after all. Isn't that what Len had been trying to tell me for so long?

But the message. Right. That was the last question, but we'd already heard the answer. At least I had...or was that just something I'd imagined? If Len was asking me about it, I must have made it up.

"Do you have a message for someone here?" My voice was stronger this time.

"As a matter of fact," the voice rattled against my breastbone. "My message is for you."

I sucked in a deep breath. That was not the answer I wanted.

Goosebumps broke out on my arms and the hairs on the back of my neck perked up like tiny antennae.

The glittering golden object resumed its steady upward, downward motion as the voice crushed the breath from my lungs.

"Be my guest."

It felt like I'd swallowed something the wrong way and was going to choke.

Sterling realized something was going on and turned on Len.

"You're freaking her out with this shit. Why did you—"

But his tirade was cut off and everything changed. My body felt as if I'd walked out of a cold shower directly into the violent winds of an ice storm.

I wrapped my arms around myself instinctively, but it didn't generate any warmth. It felt like I was tipping backward and rising into the air, like I'd been caught in an alien tractor beam.

The sounds of the theater receded away to nothing, replaced by the roaring of winds I couldn't see or feel.

In fact, I realized I couldn't see anything at all. Only the darker shadow outline of the figure, the golden something, and nothing more. Even the glowing red exit sign was gone. Something was horribly wrong.

"What happened?" I asked. "Where are we? Len, I can't see you."

There was a pause for a moment and then the weird ghost voice rattled to life again.

"This has been my home. I call it the Land of Forgetting. Don't worry. I don't expect you to remember that for long."

I was waiting for my eyes to adjust like they had in the dark theater, but it wasn't happening. It was pure darkness in all directions.

The only time I'd experienced such complete darkness was when my parents had taken me to Mammoth Cave when I was ten. The guide turned out the lights for one minute and all existence disappeared. Even though I had a parent on each side holding my hands, I'd never felt so completely alone, lost in the nothingness of absolute blackness.

Unlike in the cave, there was no sudden return of light and no one to cling to.

Another wave of cold dripped over me like someone had poured a bucket of ice water over my head in slow motion. The top of my head chilled, then it slid to my ears and nose, chin, shoulders, all the way down to my toes. For a moment, it felt like I was encased in ice, but then the extreme cold turned to a tingly burn. My entire body broke into an uncomfortable sweat, each drop pricking my skin like tiny glass shards.

Just when I thought I couldn't stand anymore, my body jolted, as sometimes happens when I'm drifting to sleep. I no longer felt anything.

"What do you want from me?"

It seemed like the being laughed, but it sounded like a robot with a synthesizer trying to simulate laughter. The effect was chilling.

"I can't express how miraculous it is to have you here, my dear. I don't recall the last conversation I had and there's certainly been no visitors. Only the teasing kind like what was happening before you got here. I don't remember much, but it hasn't stopped the longing. To be where you are, it's the only thing I desire. At last, it's going to happen!"

The voice seemed to come from everywhere and had a weird tone to it, as though it was turned up to a high frequency and had a bit of an electric zing to it. It sounded a little different every time, but always charged and not quite human.

There were a lot of words to take in and the meaning slipped away from many of them as soon as I heard them. Maybe the cold was numbing my brain.

"Who are you?" My eyes strained to see deeper into the shadow and make out some detail that would help.

"I wish I could tell you. That's one of the things I no

longer remember. What about you? Do you still know your name?"

I was about to say it, but the idea cracked to bits and floated away. Name. That's a funny word.

Not even Len could pull off a prank this elaborate and he would never do anything that would truly scare me. Thinking of Len, why wasn't he with me? I couldn't imagine why I would venture into a void like this unless Len had come along. He'd expanded my comfort zone over the years, but he was always right beside me when he did. This didn't feel right.

"You can go, Lennox is on his way." I may not have known what was going on, but I knew better than to admit I was alone. I only hoped this mysterious character wouldn't try to call my bluff.

He let out an exasperated sigh. "Lennox, you say? He hasn't been able to find his way here yet. Only you, in all this time, have been clever enough to manage that."

"Why are you hiding in the dark, and what have you done with Lennox?"

"Calm down, please. There's no need to get agitated. Lennox has not come to any harm, he simply can't get here. If I may be frank, I don't know how you managed it, but I'm very pleased you're here."

"No." The word came out of me and I focused my eyes on the glittery gold sparkle to stay grounded. "I don't want to be here. I have to go."

"Don't say that. You only just got here, and I'll be on my way soon."

I didn't like the sound of it.

"I need to get back now."

My mind reeled trying to find something to land on. I didn't understand why I was in complete darkness with a stranger. It felt like I'd just been doing something. The memory was right there, just out of reach of my consciousness.

"I'm afraid I don't know how to help you with that. If I did, I would have gone back years ago."

Years ago? Did he mean he'd been hovering around in complete darkness for years? I needed to get out of there. That was the one thing I knew for sure.

"Where are we? Why can't I see anything?"

"That's a million dollar question. One I've been pondering for a very long time. It's easier to explain where we are not. We certainly aren't in heaven, if such a place does exist. Maybe it's a holding pen. Maybe it's a dalliance before the real end. I don't know. All I know is I'd rather go back than stay here, and it's very good of you to help me."

His answer did nothing to soothe me.

"There's some mistake. I shouldn't be here at all. I need to go back where I was." There was no point telling him I couldn't remember where that was, but I still had the residual feeling of having been doing something important. Len was there. I don't know why I couldn't access what we'd been doing, but I was sure he'd been with me. I didn't like that he wasn't here now.

The shadow man chuckled, but the sound didn't have any mirth.

"I don't think you'll be able to do that."

The things he said didn't make any sense but I didn't want any clarification. The jangling sensation of dread came over me as the edges of panic began to unfurl around me.

I shivered.

"You'll get used to the cold," he said matter-of-factly. "Just don it like you would your favorite overcoat and you'll come to grips with it quicker."

He was right. The coldness was all around, not just coming in gusts. It had weight to it, but it also seemed able to move through me, as though my skin wasn't even there. The cold didn't feel harmful, it felt like me.

An image of familiar hazel eyes popped into my mind. I knew those eyes well, and I'd never wished so hard to be safe beside Lennox as I did at that moment. He'd know what to do. That was just how he was. Whatever life threw at him, he'd just roll with it somehow. What was it he'd said to me? "You act like life has all these rules, Ames, but it doesn't really. Those are just made up by people pretending to be in control. Just do what seems right to you and you'll be fine. Right? Look at me." Then he'd grinned in that devil-may-care way of his and I'd shaken my head. Of course there are rules. Society wouldn't function without them, but there was no denying Len was living proof that nothing catastrophic happened just because you chose to live life your own way.

I hoped he'd pop out of the blackness and we'd go back to what we were doing, although I just couldn't visualize what that was. Thinking felt like trying to flip through file folders that were glued together while wearing oven mitts. Was I losing my mind? Would I know if I was?

I decided to do what Len would suggest; do what felt right. Leaving felt right so I'd have to try.

"I have to get back to Lennox. I'm getting out of here."

"I hear Lennox sometimes. The woman too, but her name escapes me. They're always asking questions, but they never notice me."

So this guy was a watcher in the dark. He'd been spying on Lennox and another woman? There was no telling what he would do. I had to get out of there immediately.

The only thing I could see was still the gold sparkle, like a far off star in the depths of the universe. There had to be a way out. I did a slow turn trying to locate an exit, an object, anything that could get me out.

I just came back to the sparkle.

"Well, my charming nameless visitor, I fear it's been long enough. Would you mind holding this for me?"

The sparkle twinkled and seemed to grow a little bigger. Or maybe it was getting closer. One of those things.

"What? That?" I asked stupidly. As if he'd know I was looking at the sparkle.

The space around it had become lighter. It was indistinct but definitely something.

The object moved from side to side, as if being transferred from one hand to another. But that didn't make any sense. Who could juggle stars?

"I don't know what it is."

"You don't have to," he said. "Just keep your eye on it."

Fascinated, I did as I was instructed. As I focused completely on the glittery little orb, it seemed to increase in brightness. The area around it shimmered and parted like a veil, darkness receding to an even more opaque blackness behind it. In between the two heavy saturations of dark was a flickering lightness. A gentle gray in between black. At first, it was still, and the sparkle was just a single point of light. Then my eyes acclimated to this new way of seeing. The shadow of the man I'd been seeing was resolving into something more. More than a shape. It was a fuzzy image of a man. It had a grainy quality, like a very old clip from the dawn of film. It even jumped and skipped as if coming through an old projector with a deteriorating film strip. The only thing that remained constant was the glowing glimmer of light. I could now see that the man was cradling it in his hands.

I looked on and noticed more and more details. At first, the man's eyes were cast down at the glittery orb, but as I stared at his face, trying to work out if I knew him, he raised his gaze to meet mine. The instant our eyes met, alarm bells went off in my head. Words were leaving me, but the way he looked at me made me defensive. It was a wild, desperate look and as uncomfortable as the intensity of his stare made me, I couldn't risk looking away.

The longer I stared at him, the brighter he became. Details were starting to resolve themselves, although the lines and pops like film distortion were still present. His outfit was old fashioned. It looked like he was wearing a long sleeved white blouse with the cuffs unbuttoned and rolled up to his elbows. There was a dark vest over the shirt and dark pants. A tie was loosened and slightly askew at his neck.

As he regarded me, a wolfish smile spread across his gray lips. He fidgeted with the glitter orb, passing it back and forth from hand to hand. As he did so, the orb seemed to increase and decrease in size and shift from a silvery color to a warmer yellow and back again. It was such an usual sight that I turned my attention to it.

"It's pretty isn't it?" He held the sparkle up.

"Yes." I agreed. "Pretty."

"Wait until you see what it can do."

He raised his cupped hands to his lips and blew on the sparkle. In response, a shower of tiny light fragments rose from it and filled the air. They spun up and around us and all over the blank space we were in. In an instant, it looked like we were enclosed in a sparkly sheer net of static. It seemed as though someone had spun a delicate lace out of light and draped it at the periphery of what could be seen. Only he and I were inside this glittering area. Beyond, things were dull and muddy in dark shades of indigo and black. If I really concentrated on what was past the lights, it seemed that shadowy figures were moving around, but I didn't want to focus on that. The sparkles were too beautiful.

Like floating in a lake at night. I had a sense of endlessness. Past, present, and future were all around me, but not in a chaotic or linear way. It was comforting.

"This is nice," I said.

"Yes," he murmured. "Would you like to stay awhile?"

It was so beautiful, I couldn't imagine going anywhere

else. A dull sense of alarm pulsed through my mind, but it was secondary to the wonder at our surroundings.

"You know," he looked at me earnestly. "There's something I'd dearly love to share with you."

"Hmm?"

"How would you like a little gold?"

He held up the sparkle, which was glowing a warm golden yellow, brighter than ever, even though he'd blown so many sparks off it to decorate our space.

"Catch!" he called and tossed it up. It seemed to fly at me from the hazy center of a dark tunnel. Firefly sparks swirling all around it. Maybe it was coming toward me. Maybe I was moving toward it. However it was happening, the sparkle and I would intersect with each other.

Even though I'd never seen such a wondrous thing, my arms instinctively stretched out in front of me as the object got closer. When it reached my fingertips, reality changed. The thing I was reaching for split into countless golden pinpricks of light. I watched in slow-motion wonder as the opaque confines of my own body did the same. It would appear that I had morphed into a shadow person too. There was nothing more than a deep black outline of the body I'd had. Like the dawn of a universe, my shadow fingers swept away in a galactic haze. My hands followed suit. My wrists. It was mesmerizing to see. The vague sense of being in my body that I'd always taken for granted was replaced with a sensation I'd never felt before. It was cold, so very cold, but I felt like I was opening up. Joining the current of unknown existence. I was everything, everywhere, nothing, and nowhere all at the same time.

A fluttering sensation started in my chest and it seemed like I was tilting somehow.

"It's a fair trade!" he bellowed as if very far away. "A life for a life!"

He laughed and laughed, the sound filling my head as my

eyes stared in awe at the transformation I was undergoing. As his laughter grew stronger and clearer, I noticed that my glowing cells weren't just fanning out into the ether. They were flowing to him. Every brilliant speck of mine that broke off was adding to his increasing brightness.

"Wha—" I tried to ask what he was doing, but the word wouldn't even form for me anymore.

"Do you have a question, my dear?" He stopped laughing long enough to ask. "No matter. You'll be out of energy soon and have more than enough time to ponder all your questions here."

The words caught somewhere in the back of my mind and prickled there. I couldn't quite access what they all meant at the moment. It couldn't have been a conscious thing, because my thoughts were getting fuzzier by the moment, but the primal urge to survive took over.

"St—" I tried to speak again but the word wouldn't come.

I'd been so caught up in watching myself unravel that I hadn't noticed how vibrant he'd become. He shone with bright colors and his edges were sharply defined against the murky darkness behind and around him. His eyes glowed a bright blue. His lips were a lovely shade of pink. He seemed like a thing of beauty, and I smiled as the tips of my hair began to sparkle off toward him.

The coldness that filled me became more intense as he grew brighter and stronger. I didn't know how to fight, although I understood that I wanted to. Trying to anchor myself to that feeling, I needed to summon whatever strength I had left to reverse this process. Wishing for some sort of miracle, a tiny sensation of warmth pressed into my chest. Next, there was a phantom sensation of a warm hand wrapped around my cold one...although visually, my hands had already turned to glittering stardust and floated away.

The warmth was comforting, but it was nearly finished

then. I couldn't think of anything to do and all that was left was my hair, halfway gone already. I couldn't see my own face, but that must be next and then the transformation would be complete.

As I watched the last of my hair spiral away, like a double helix of tiny galaxies, the sense of warmth spread throughout the space my body used to occupy. I could hear something that seemed familiar, but I couldn't place it. An image of hazel eyes flitted across my remaining consciousness, peaking my interest.

Sound rustled into the memory of my ears.

"Amy! AMY! Wake up! Please, Amy!"

They were interesting sounds. Amy sounded familiar, tickling at the edges of my mind.

"Don't listen to that," the man said. "It's too late for you. It's my time now."

I didn't have the energy to respond. It didn't make sense to me anyway, but the small voice was persistent.

"Amy, do not let go. You have to remember who you are."

There was that sound again...Amy. It felt like something powerful. Something I knew.

The sparkles from my hair were moving in slow motion now. I guess there were still some left.

"You are Amy Jean Morrison and you are the most important person in my life. Do you remember that?"

Familiarity pulsed around me. Amy Jean Morrison. I knew that combination of sounds. And that voice. It was very low and quiet, but I knew it too. It had my attention.

"Amy, do you remember that time in ninth grade? I convinced you to cut class with me, even though you really didn't want to. But you did because I told you we were just going to come back to my house so we could watch Alfred Hitchcock movies. Remember how scared you were? You just knew we'd get caught, and you thought Hitchcock would scare you too much. I insisted you would love it, and we wouldn't get in trouble, and you finally caved because you trusted me."

The voice caught, like it was suddenly in great pain.

One of my sparkles stopped in mid flow to the man and hovered between us.

He saw it instantly.

"No!" he bellowed.

Unlike the little voice I was hearing, this man was much louder. The sound thundered over me like being pummeled by a boulder.

The sparkle shuddered for a moment and slowly started back on its journey toward the man.

All my sparkles would be gone soon. Then I'd be able to rest. How calm and quiet that would be.

But the small voice came back. Even quieter than before but still clear enough for me to hear.

"Amy, please don't give up. I need you to remember who you are, okay? I can't do life without you, Ames. You're the only person who knows me, and I love you so much."

Ames. Amy.

The pieces clicked into place and understanding came back. *I* was Amy. That distant voice was Lennox. I didn't remember how we'd gotten separated, but this was wrong. I wasn't in the right place, and I needed to get back to Lennox.

All at once, it felt like someone simultaneously pressed the rewind button and dropped a lava-hot elephant on my chest.

"I'm Amy," I said, my memories flooding back to me as if a dam had burst. "I'm ghost hunting with Len. We're hunting *you*! You don't get to have my life."

"I told you not to listen to him!" The former shadow man had transformed again. He was bigger and brighter than ever, his eyes golden with light like two blazing suns. "It's my turn to go back! You stay here now!"

"No!" Warmth flowed through me, dispelling the cold nothingness that had nearly overtaken me. "You had your turn. My life is for me!"

Cross over. A female voice tickled my mind, vaguely familiar. Meaning was still a little fuzzy, but this made sense. Ghosts need to cross over. This one was trying to come back, but it was a one way ticket. If he wanted to leave wherever we were, he'd have to go the other direction, but I had no idea where that was or how to push him in that direction.

"You need to cross over." I hoped Len and the female could hear me in the same way I could hear them. If I was lucky, they could help me do what needed to be done. Maybe I should have watched scarier movies with Len. At least I would have had an idea of where to start. The only thing I knew from being adjacent to ghost culture was "go toward the light," only that didn't apply here since the only light was a gold glittering ball that was apparently energy.

While I was desperately looking for some clue, I noticed that the gold particles that had so rapidly unraveled from me and built up the ghost were now flowing away from him and back to me. I was feeling stronger and more aware, but his eyes were still shining with a cold energy I recognized as fury.

Ghost movies capitalize on the moaning wails of ghosts to elicit a quick scare, but they sound like a lullaby compared to the real sound of rage and anguish that blasted out of this being. Whatever realm we were in did not obey the laws of life on my earthly dimension. I could see the shock waves as misty distortions emanating from his gaping mouth. I watched them barreling toward me with panicky dread. What would happen to me when those waves hit? I'd already had the particles of my being whisked away, there was no telling what other things he was capable of doing.

"Help!" I cried, desperate for Lennox to hear me somehow. "I don't know what to do!"

The cataclysmic roar coming from the ghost vibrated through my consciousness. It was even more difficult to hear what I needed to, but I managed to get a snippet of an answer.

"We need to open a bridge."

It wasn't Len's voice, but the female again. With a snap of clarity I realized it must be Emlynn. I had a team of two to help me defeat this ghost. That was something.

Even though I wasn't in a physical state, I still had the impulse to duck to avoid the waves coming my way.

Awareness of my circumstances seemed to sharpen my mind, even though I had no body to maneuver, I was able to "move" through space in a manner of speaking. Without the limits of physicality, I was able to move like a wave myself. Where the rage waves crested, I made a trough.

"A bridge?" I asked. "How?"

The moment of concentration it took to process what Emlynn said and respond cost me a smooth avoidance of an incoming wave. The edge of one crashed into my hand and made its presence known as immediate pain. My thumb burned with intense fire.

I cried out. I wanted to protect my injured hand somehow but I had to stay focused on the battery of waves so I wouldn't suffer anything worse.

"Amy!" I could hear Len again. His voice was laced with anguish. "Stay with me, Amy. We're going to get you out of there!"

Hearing him again calmed me, despite the pain, but I had to concentrate on not getting hit again, and I still didn't know what I could do about the bridge Emlynn mentioned.

"Vade in pace. Intra requiem tuam. Vade in pace. Intra requiem tuam."

Emlynn started chanting in Latin.

The weight of everything that was going on closed in around me. The ghost's wailing was the main sound in my head. I was trying to hear whispers from Len and Emlynn, while maintaining absolute concentration on the relentless volley of waves so they didn't annihilate me.

I didn't know Latin, and it wasn't the optimum time to carefully process each syllable Emlynn was saying.

It helped only a little when Len's voice joined the chant.

My senses already at overload, I noticed a ray of white light flickering into existence behind the ghost. His attention was focused on me.

"Amy! Say it. Vade in pace!" Len took a quick break from his chanting to urge me to action.

While concentrating on Len's voice, I missed the tail of a wave that caught me in the foot.

I couldn't take more hits like that. My thumb still felt like it was a pot of boiling water and now my foot was suffering the same fate. If we didn't get the ghost over the bridge fast I was going to lose.

"Vade in pace," I said. "Intra requiem tuam."

I joined the mantra as best I could while still continuing to anticipate the coming waves.

With my voice joining theirs, the white light grew brighter and larger.

I spoke with more conviction after a few repetitions. I was getting the rhythm of the unfamiliar words.

Finally, the ghost seemed to understand that something was happening. He paused his onslaught of sound and shock waves and turned to look behind him.

In that moment of respite, I launched forward, still chanting, and attempted to see if one spirit can push another one into a bridge of light.

I gasped as fiery breath filled my lungs.

"She's waking up! Give her space!"

I didn't realize my eyes were closed until they fluttered

open. Everything was blurry and confusing. There were faces hovering over me, wide-eyes, grim mouths.

There was a hard, coldness beneath my legs, back, and head. Was I on the floor? But a warm, light, pressure rested on my chest, and my left hand was gripped tight.

My right hand and left foot throbbed in pain.

"It hurts," I mumbled.

"She's talking!"

I slowly refocused my eyes on what I thought the source of the voice was. A man and a woman knelt next to me. The man had his hand pressed to my chest. The woman was holding my hand and the man's other hand, joining the three of us together. He had beautiful hazel eyes. Once I saw the tracks of eyeliner tears on his face, reality came back to me.

"Len. What happened?"

A sound somewhere between a laugh and a sob choked out of him, and he moved his hand from my chest to grasp my free hand.

"Are you okay, Ames?"

The woman's eyes had been closed, but she opened them and gently placed my hand on the ground beside me. Now that my senses were coming back to me, I remembered that she was Emlynn. Part of the ghost hunting group. That's what I'd been doing...ghost hunting with Len.

"You managed to get caught up with an energy stealer," Emlynn said. The words were matter-of-fact, but her voice was weak. "I've never experienced anything like that before. That was intense, and I was only experiencing it secondhand. How are you feeling, Amy?"

I felt like I'd just woken up from a nightmare. Bits and pieces played on repeat in my mind's eye, but some details were already fading away.

"Tired," I said, suddenly struck with a bone-tired exhaustion I hadn't felt since I'd had mono in high school.

"I couldn't believe it." This was a different voice I recognized. I looked up and noticed Sterling standing behind Len. If there was one thing I'd learned about Sterling and Carlisle, they were always composed. The Sterling standing in the theater had rumpled hair, his face drawn into a long frown of worry. His eyes were wide and gazing toward me, although I didn't get the impression he was really seeing me.

"At first I thought you and Len had hatched a plan to make it all more convincing, although that's not like you. But you went into a sort of trance, and then even I knew you weren't faking. Carlisle was screaming for someone to do something, but none of us had any idea what to do. But then someone did."

He turned his somewhat blank stare to the back of Len's head and pointed at him.

"This kid. My ridiculous, screw-up brother knew exactly what to do. He told me to call 911, then ran out, got her—" he gestured to Emlynn, "And they made this crazy connection circle. I didn't think it would do anything, but it did. You're back now."

Emlynn shot Len a glance then looked up at Sterling.

"I think you need a drink," she said.

Sterling ignored her and put a hand on Len's shoulder.

"We all think we'll be the hero in a crisis, but look at all of us. We choked. You got right into gear, and you did it. You were amazing!"

I don't know what was more shocking, having been pulled into a ghost realm with a spirit trying to steal my life force, or hearing Sterling compliment his brother.

Lennox didn't take his eyes off me.

"Thanks," he said. "But we're not done yet. You and Carlisle go out front so you can direct EMS when they get here."

I'd never seen Sterling and Carlisle move so fast or Len be so authoritative with his brothers.

"EMS is coming?" I asked, still sounding feeble.

"Yeah. You cracked your head pretty good when you fell on the floor. Best not to take any chances with that."

"Oh." I turned my attention to the back of my head to see if I felt any pain, but all I felt was the hard floor under me.

Now that I sort of knew what I'd just been through, Emlynn, Len, and I took turns looking at each other. Finally Emlynn stood up.

"I'm going to leave you guys alone right now, but someone needs to tell you your 'best friends' schtick is a bunch of bull-shit. The things I felt from you two while we were connected was way beyond friendship. You may have been in denial this long, but newsflash, you're in love with each other." She started to walk away, leaving me and Len to gape at each other.

"You're welcome," Emlynn called before I heard her pull the theater door open and disappear.

I knew we wouldn't be alone for long with EMS on the way. I had to act fast.

"Len." His name was like velvet in my mouth, smooth and heavy. Luxurious but familiar.

I searched his face, and it was like my trip to the beyond had removed the veil I'd had over my own eyes for most of my life.

His face was always pale, but it was paler than usual. There was no hiding from the black streaks leading from his eyes all down his cheeks. He may have been a master of masking his feelings so he wouldn't get hurt, but I'd always thought I'd seen through it all. To the bright, golden heart that beat within his scrawny chest. I'd been wrong. I'd also been extremely stupid.

In the muffled distance, the piercing wail of a siren could be heard. I realized it must be coming for me, so I only had a few more moments alone with Len, and I needed to make the most of them.

Len slipped his hand gently into mine. He looked me in the eye. I could tell he was trying so hard to hide his fear and be strong for me and the realization nearly made my heart burst.

"I'm so sorry," he blurted out, his eyes filling with fresh tears. "I never would have asked you to come here if I thought something could actually happen to you. I promised to keep you safe, and I completely failed." His voice broke and he looked away from me.

"Hey," I said. "Nobody would have guessed this would happen. I wasn't even sure any of this stuff was real."

"But I knew," Len said, snapping his gaze back to me. "I knew it was real, and I knew there could be bad stuff, but I just assumed it wouldn't happen here. You mean more to me than anybody, Amy. You never did care for this kind of stuff. I shouldn't have asked you, and I'm sorry."

All I wanted to do was wrap Len in a big hug, so I started to push up but Len stilled me.

"Take it easy, Ames. You've been through a lot."

The siren was getting louder. There wasn't time to be cautious.

"Len, I have to tell you something." I didn't want to be laying on the floor of a theater while having a serious conversation so I pushed myself up slowly. This time, Len cradled my head and we gently moved together as I got into a sitting position.

"Do you feel ok? Lean on me if you're dizzy."

I did feel a little dizzy, but not from any head injuries.

Len put his arm around my shoulders and slid right next to me.

"You have to listen to me," I insisted. "EMS is going to be here soon."

"Of course," he said. "I'm listening."

He turned his face to mine and we were only a couple inches from each other. I caught his eye again and resisted the urge to just stare into his beautiful eyes. They were eyes I'd looked into so many times in our lives, but it was different this time. They were all I wanted to see.

"I was on the other side. It was completely dark and so cold. This guy was talking to me. I couldn't see anything other than a sparkle of light, but do you know what kept me from panicking?"

Len's lips were trembling but he didn't say anything.

"You," I said. "All I could think about was you and what you'd do and how much I wanted to be with you. Now that Emlynn's said it, she's completely right. I always want to be with you Len. Ever since I met you, until today, into tomorrow. I wanted to get back here to be with you. You know I love you, that's not a surprise, but that's not all. I'm in love with you too. And I really hope you feel the same, because if you don't—"

I didn't get a chance to finish babbling.

"I hope this isn't a concussion talking," Len said, "because I've been in love with you since day one, Amy."

The doors to the theater were opening. I didn't break my gaze from Len's and did the only thing that felt right.

As his brothers held the doors to the theater so EMS could push a stretcher inside, I closed my eyes and pressed my lips against Len's. He wrapped me firm, but gentle, in his arms and kissed me back. Years of repressed emotion, on both sides, danced across our lips. Maybe I was still messed up from crossing to the other side, but those dazzling sparkles I'd seen there had nothing on the fireworks going off in my heart while we kissed.

Vaguely conscious of the paramedics, I pulled away. Len

and I had only a few seconds to look into each other's eyes, but I squeezed his hand quickly.

"We should have done that a long time ago."

He coughed out a kind of incredulous laugh.

"Yeah, ya think?"

The stolen moment was truly over as a paramedic crouched next to me and asked my name and if I could tell him what had happened.

As he proceeded to check my vitals, Len and I just looked at each other, stupid grins on our faces.

The back of my head was starting to throb, but warmth was returning to my body. All this time, I'd been afraid of ghosts because I thought they might haunt my house or steal my soul. I'd never considered that the threat of losing everything could show me exactly what I had.

The paramedics decided it would be best to get me checked out at the hospital and have some tests run. They strapped me into the stretcher as Len's brothers stood off to the side looking stricken. Meanwhile, Len and I just gazed at each other with a newfound awe.

Before they got ready to wheel me away, Len squeezed my hand. "Will you go on an official date with me next weekend?"

I wanted to frown and pretend to think it over carefully, but my head was actually starting to hurt.

"Yeah, but I have one condition."

"Anything," Len said, looking gravely serious.

"Let me pick the event this time."

ACKNOWLEDGMENTS

This story would not exist if I'd never met Ken Suminski. Thank you for getting me out to that first public ghost hunt, which has since turned to several. Luckily, I never ended up like Amy.

Thank you to my husband and children, who graciously put up with all the time and energy I spend on writing.

Heather Hollister, you are incredible! I can't thank you enough for all your expert help over the years.

ABOUT THE AUTHOR

S.J. Lomas is a cheerful Michigan girl who writes strange and somewhat dark stories.

She's written a YA duology about dreamworlds, conspiracy, friendship, and romance: Dream Girl, Dream Frequency. She's also contributed to the first Winter Chills collection and has two books of poetry: The Blue Muse, In Between: Poems of Midlife.

She does author interviews at her website:
www.sjlomas.com

DEAD AIR

DAN MACDONALD

I t started when I was a little boy. Specifically, when I got sick.

I found out I could hear voices.

I think I always could, but they got much louder when I started paying attention.

To hear them, you must listen.

Listen to the sound of the room and then listen beyond that.

The fridge humming. The furnace purring.

The creak of the house shifting.

The birds in the trees. The cars on the streets.

The wind touching the window.

The snow coming down. There is a sound to it if you listen closely.

And then listen deeper than that.

It's the other things that make a different kind of noise.

Perhaps before you go to sleep at night, when you're alone and there's nothing else to listen to, to distract you.

"It's like a radio playing in another room."

That's how someone once described it, the things I hear every night.

It made sense when they put it that way.

The person who said it was supposedly psychic. A celebrated clairvoyant on some random daytime TV talk show I saw when I was much younger, home sick watching all the shows I normally missed because I was in school.

The psychic was a large, robust woman, massive forearms, and husky hands. Despite her well-manicured nails, they looked like they were hands that had seen their fair share of hard work over the years.

Her hefty figure was draped in a loose, flowing dress. She was dripping in gaudy jewellery, gold rings, beaded bracelets, charms that dangled from her ears and wrists; a bit on the eccentric side.

Also, clearly no stranger to a tanning salon.

She had a natural kindness, easy to see her as a counsellor or "life coach" of some sort, maybe a bedside nurse or perhaps most fittingly: a warm waitress at a diner. Smoker's voice. Raspy laugh. Rough around the edges. Lines traced across her face like a road map illustrating a rocky journey of hard living. Despite her kindness, she was someone who appeared to have zero patience for BS and would have no problem telling you what's what, without hesitation, if you needed to hear it.

The TV show audience was made up of curious people who wanted to know about dead relatives, the afterlife, their future. Perhaps people desperate to make sense of things that made no sense.

People who so badly wanted to believe.

A woman from the audience was selected to ask the psychic a question. She was a beaming conservative-looking mom, who appeared ecstatic for her fifteen minutes of fame.

She stood up with her young son—about eleven —and nervously but eagerly informed the psychic: "I'm a really big fan! This is my son and he hears dead people, just like the kid in that movie! He hears them talking!"

There was a ripple of amused chuckles through the audience.

The psychic remained stone faced as she directed her question to the child.

"Do you hear the voices loud and clear...or is it hard to tune in to what they're saying?" she asked him.

"Hard to hear them," the little boy answered, timidly.

The psychic nodded knowingly, as if she had an immediate understanding of what it was he was experiencing.

"It's like a radio playing in another room on low? Like you can barely make out the words, but you can still hear people talkin'? Right honey?"

He nodded.

She continued.

"It's like...you know you can hear *something*... but you can't quite make it out. Right? You have to strain. But the harder you listen, the harder it gets to hear. It's because those sounds, those voices *aren't* on the radio in another room. They are playin' through the little radio antenna inside your head, sweetie. You're tuning in to *something*, and you need to learn how to tune in *clearer*. That's a skill and it takes time and practice before you get it. And hey, maybe you never will. Maybe this is as clear as it'll ever get. Maybe some things will tune in better than others. You know how on a clear day you get better reception on the radio or TV? Other days you get nothing? Just static and snow? It might be like that. You've got it though. Listen to those voices. If you can make anything out, pay attention to what they're telling you, because they're reaching out for a reason, okay? But be careful too, hon. Don't invite any unwanted guests in, if you know what I mean.

"You just have to be careful they aren't malicious. But listening won't hurt you."

I never forgot that TV show or what the psychic said because it made sense to me.

I never realized I have what that kid has, until I saw it spelled out on that stupid daytime talk show.

It's not as crazy as it sounds, and even more than that, I'm convinced *everyone* has a little bit of whatever...this...is.

My belief is we all have it, it's just that most of us don't pay any attention to it. We aren't listening for it, so we don't hear it. Or maybe it's harder to decipher amongst all the noise, the static, the fuzz.

And on the other hand, maybe some of us pay too much attention to it and it drives us to darker places.

We see those people every day. They are the ones on street corners having conversations with no one. Perhaps the voices just got too loud to ignore? Too amplified and focused to drown out.

And maybe it's not the voices that drove them there at all. Perhaps they have lost their mind or are on drugs. Maybe a combo of the two. You can snuff out the static through many methods and many people take substances to block out, erase, distract and forget.

That said: I don't believe what I hear is just a matter of me losing my mind, and I know it's not drugs.

What I experience is something else.

It's a constant running commentary, conversations, words, questions.

It's something I'm tuning into or something that is tuning in to me.

Some of it is just our own internal voice, the stream of consciousness that narrates every single human being's every waking moment as we go about life.

Usually, it's a version of our own voice or someone we know.

Our intuition. Our consciousness.

But there is another layer that's constantly flowing like a steady current or undertow in an ever-moving river underneath it all.

For me, I can barely hear it and I'm barely aware of it. My brain tunes it out very easily, but it's always there.

It's exactly like what that daytime talk show psychic said: It's like a radio playing in another room. Like that tiny boombox I had when I was a kid back in the 80s. I dropped that mini boombox in my room once and the antenna snapped off.

After that it was difficult to get reception.

"It just sounds like snow," my dad would say.

Snow.

Ghosts of radio waves, static-riddled whispers of broadcasts that would drift in and out as I'd grow more and more frustrated, trying to position the radio or manipulate the stub of the broken antenna with tin foil or a wire closet hanger to pick up a better signal. At times my broken radio would pick up some great reception and tune in crystal clear.

Mostly, since the antenna was broken, radio broadcasts would be barely audible, combined with indecipherable static, fusing with other stations and sounding like jumbled nonsense. Sometimes the transmissions came in so low I had to sit with my ear right at the speaker to catch what was coming through.

The sounds I hear in my head, those other sounds, the voices, are just like that and they come through with the best reception at night.

It's not remotely scary or creepy.

For the most part, it's just nonsense and in a weird way, it's comforting.

The same way one might find comfort in white noise, a running fan, a humidifier; the constant murmur lulls me to sleep. Sometimes I pick up what the voices are saying and for the most part, it's like eavesdropping in on a conversation that you're not a part of and know nothing about.

Like a game of broken telephone.

I always go to bed before Sarah. She stays downstairs, a night owl.

We are that couple who goes to bed at different times. It sounds dysfunctional, but it works. After eleven years together, you need to develop a routine that works, and this is ours.

I head upstairs to bed around 10 p.m. She stays up online, reading news, watching TV.

A night person.

Every night it's mostly the same thing.

I slip into bed, turn the bedroom and upstairs hall light off with the app on my phone, and roll over onto my side.

I close my eyes and begin the gentle drift into sleep.

And while sleep creeps up slowly, I listen.

The silence and stillness and maybe even the darkness helps with reception.

It's always so random. Just snippets. Conversation fragments.

Tonight, as I drift into sleep, I'm tuned in.

And they are in full chatter.

"...if she could just focus she'd be fine, but she doesn't want to, so I don't know what to do!"

"...wouldn't have to tell me twice, hell, I'd be out the door if I were you..."

"...you don't know her like I know her though, it's not that easy to just leave...and I can't just send her somewhere else..."

It sounded, from what I could gather, like two women talking about ...a daughter? A sister? Perhaps a mother? Maybe a lover or spouse? I have no idea and I never will.

That's the thing about any conversations I hear. They are never resolved. I never fully know what they're about.

They just float in, already in session, and fade out never to return, like a storm cloud forming and dissipating.

Are they dead people? Are they someone else's thoughts? Am I some kind of mutant with super-hearing, and I'm over-hearing the neighbours? I honestly have no idea.

I feel my body relax as sleep creeps up on me.

I listen some more. Different voices now. An older man.

"...all this used to be grapes. I was growing grapes here and would make wine. Wasn't any good as a wine maker though. Used to give it to the mailman. Not even sure if he liked it or not. I'd drink it, but I drink anything. He could use it to clean his drain for all I know! But the grapes are gone now. Stopped growing them..."

Sleep tugs on me gently, pulling me deeper. The closer I get to sleep, the clearer the voices become.

A younger voice now. Not sure if it's male or female.

"...broke some dishes trying to make breakfast for my mom and blamed it on my dad...he told me not to try to climb up on the countertop unless I asked him first...stupid dishes..."

Nonsense.

And then sleep takes me.

————

I awoke suddenly in the night to the sound of the front door downstairs violently slamming shut.

I froze. My first thought was that Sarah went out for a cigarette, but then I felt her weight, heard her breathing beside me.

Wait a minute, I thought to myself.

Who the fuck just shut the front door? Was someone leav-

*ing? Were we just robbed in our sleep and that was the intruder,
shutting the door on their way out?*

Or is someone still here, downstairs?

I held my breath, straining to listen for anything. A creak
on the floor, shuffling around, whispering downstairs.

Nothing but a thick silence.

A small snap. *The house settling? Too small a noise to be
someone moving around.*

I reached for my phone on the charger on the night table
and pulled up the app that controls the lights and turned on
all the downstairs lamps.

As the lamps switched on downstairs, some of the light
trickled up the stairs into the hallway outside our bedroom
door.

I listened.

More silence.

If someone was down there, they would have reacted to
the lights suddenly turning on. They'd have jumped. Shouted
out. Scurried and run out, realizing they were caught.

Something.

But I already knew there was no one down there.

I listened longer, for anything.

Sarah's breathing beside me.

3:43 a.m.

It was sinking in now: The door did not slam shut. That
unmistakeable sound of our heavy door closing was another
noise in my head. It was a dream. My imagination.

I knew without worrying too much about it that if I went
downstairs right now to check things out, (like they do in
horror movies and it never ends well) our door would be
bolted shut just as Sarah had left it when she came in after her
final smoke of the night.

There was no need to worry. I've had this dream before.

In fact, I hear that exact sound of the door slamming shut

(it's not actually "slamming" at all, it just sounds like a slam the way the noise carries up the stairs) every single night before Sarah comes to bed. I hear it whether I'm awake in bed or not. It's the last thing she does before coming up. She shuts the door and locks it. The noise is ground into my psyche, so naturally I had a dream about it.

That's all this was.

I flicked the downstairs lights off with the app, put my phone back on the charger and rolled over onto my side.

I heard a car drive by outside. The whispery whoosh as it passed by our house and faded away out of earshot.

And quiet. I listened as I closed my eyes.

There was no one downstairs.

"...love what you did with the paint colour in here, it's gorgeous..."

The chatter was still going. And it melted into the quiet of the house and the small, normal noises that a house makes in the middle of the night. That's all there was.

Nothing more.

———

"Jim, you gotta get up. Jim? Your alarm is going off..."

Not sure if it was Sarah or my alarm that woke me, but I was up.

7 a.m. always came so fast.

I grabbed my phone and hit the dismiss button, killing the alarm. Sarah didn't work until 10 a.m. so she had a few more merciful hours of sleep than me. I got up and started the routine.

Into the bathroom.

Down the stairs, noted casually that the front door was bolted as I knew it would be, through the living room and into the kitchen.

Handful of vitamins. Big glass of water. Hit the button on the coffee machine. Went upstairs to take a shower.

Then off to work. Normal day.

I started to put together a mental "to do list" of things I needed to get done at work today and I heard a wee bit more of the chatter as the shower hit my face.

"...doesn't even know what he's doing..."

"...oh my god... that's terrifying..."

"...he's going to die..."

Who is going to die? Unsettling. Like the door slamming shut last night.

I corrected myself: the *dream* of the door slamming shut last night.

Just nonsense in the brain.

Turned the shower off. Time to get dressed and start the day.

———

I got home from work at about 4:45, a time of day I was never a fan of. Even worse in late winter, when it still wouldn't be spring for another month or so.

The light always bothered me around this time. I was so much more of a morning person.

Morning light is fresh and crisp. Hopeful, cheerful and bright. Energizing.

The light this time of day was different.

The mood is always uncomfortable in the late afternoon before dusk. The sun is getting ready to begin its descent. Cold, dying daylight pours in at a strange angle from the west, casting ugly light and tall shadows. Wasn't very motivating.

I was tired from work, seven hours of sitting in front of a computer all day and coming home to a sun that's equally tired of being out. It feels like the day is basically over.

Sarah would be home about an hour after me.

I always found it unsettling, coming home to an empty house. Never liked it. Feels so cold.

I opened the curtains wide, letting that sour winter afternoon light in.

I plopped on the couch and grabbed the book I was reading, but kept it on my lap.

Chatter. Voices. Conversations in progress. They came through loud and clear in the quiet house during these lonely afternoons.

"...gotta clean all the gutters out and it's a mess..."

"...well I know the streets better than anyone, I've been navigating this city since the fifties..."

I coughed loudly and sneezed. A slight headache was forming. I was just about to get up to grab an allergy pill or a cold med in case it was an oncoming bug, and then the tone changed:

"...Jim, you there? ...Jim?"

Loud and clear. Clearer than the others. And it felt... pointed. Aside from the voice saying my name – it felt stronger, directed at me. Direct broadcast for my ears.

It was a woman's voice, familiar, but no one I could put a name or face to.

I listened. Faded scraps of conversations, nothing I could make out well. I was trying to hear that voice again.

The quiet was heavy in the house. Almost tense.

I listened.

"...hi Jim..."

I held my breath.

There she was. I tried not to overthink it, tried not to listen too hard. You know those magic eye puzzles that used to come in the paper, in the comic section? To properly see whatever picture was hidden in the puzzle, you almost had to let your eyes go out of focus and not stare at any one specific spot? That's what it's like listening. You can't home in too closely. You must listen in general and let whatever comes through, come through.

I responded back with my own internal voice, even though I felt a bit ridiculous. Hearing voices is one thing. Talking back to them is another.

"...are you talking to me?" I asked.

Immediately the voice responded.

"...be careful and don't make any mistakes, Jim..."

Was I imagining this? It sure didn't feel like it. This felt like another party, another person dialing in and messaging me directly.

"...not sure what you mean..." I thought back at them.

Nothing. A car drove by outside. The furnace came on.

"...hello? Are you there..." I asked into my own thoughts.

Nothing but the thick silence of a winter afternoon.

Be careful and don't make any mistakes. I chuckled to myself.

Okay. I'll try not to. Weird.

Decided to nap until Sarah got home. My head was pounding. Could be the pressure change. Could be that seasonal headache that everyone gets this time of year. My Dad used to say it felt like he was wearing a hat that was too tight, the pressure got so bad. For my mom and sister it was all in the chest.

My dad and I, it always got to our heads. A nap would help.

But first, I had to grab that sinus pill.

You must stay ahead of these winter bugs.

———

It was a typical evening. We watched mindless TV, flipped around for a movie, and found nothing as usual and ended up half-reading news and scrolling through social media.

In the back of my head was the message I heard earlier. It felt like a warning, but what intrigued me even more was the clarity with which it had come through.

"...*be careful and don't make any mistakes, Jim...*"

Crystal clear. Strong.

I've heard these voices and this chatter my whole life, but never before directly to me. This no longer felt like listening in on a conversation in progress. This felt like a direct call.

What did I have to lose? I decided to humour myself and do a search online.

Searching the words "Hearing Voices" leads to all kinds of sites about mental health. They say it's not necessarily mental illness and that it's a common thing for many people to experience what professionals call "auditory hallucinations."

I thought of the sound of the door slamming last night. I have those all the time.

But the voices. Those are something else.

I changed my search.

"Hearing+Voices+Mediums+Psychics."

My thoughts turned to the psychic, the clairvoyant who I saw on that talk show when I was a kid.

I typed the word "clairvoyant" into the search bar.

Turns out that's not the correct word I was looking for when it comes to a person who can hear voices, like a psychic. Clairvoyant is seeing things.

Amazing what you learn when you consult the great and powerful internet.

The proper term, I learned, is clairaudient.

Clairaudience is the ability to hear psychic messages. According to the site these may be external, coming from a source outside your head, or may be internal. A voice in your head.

I searched "How to develop clairaudience."

Skimming through lots of the new age talk, I found a few suggestions on how to better tune in to these voices.

The article suggested listening. I already knew that.

But the article stressed making an effort to gently tune into sounds you normally don't focus on – leaves rustling, distant wind chimes, traffic – and see if you can isolate each one and focus on it for a few moments.

"At first, this may be hard, but when you practice doing this more often, you will expand your range of hearing and it will be easier for you to pick up sounds from the spirit world."

I chuckled to myself.

The spirit world.

The second suggestion in the article was to ask questions.

"Ask into the beyond for an auditory message. Are you pondering a specific question? Focus on it and ask about it. You must call out to the beyond. Invite them in, tell them they are welcome, that you are listening, that you are receptive."

It echoed part of what the talk show psychic had said to the kid:

"If you can make anything out, pay attention to what they're telling you."

I wasn't specifically looking for guidance on anything, but I decided to give it a try that night in bed.

"Invite them in…"

———

I was on my side, eyes closed, the faint light from Sarah watching TV creeping up the stairs.

I focused on the sound of the furnace. The odd car that would drive by. The wind.

The small ticking of the blinds against the window from the furnace air coming through the vent.

And I did what the site suggested and "called out to the beyond" so to speak.

Alright... if you're there, whoever you are. Come through. This is my invite to you. Tell me what you want. Tell me who you are. Come in and talk to me. This is your invitation. Show me what you've got.

I internally eye-rolled myself. But I listened, eyes closed. Murmurs. Noise.

Come in. Show me.

I want to know who you are.

And then:

"Jim."

That same voice I heard earlier said my name. Again.

Not a question. A notification.

It was telling me it was here.

Who is this? I asked in my head.

"Jim..." it said again. Silence. And then, eerily low, taut, cautious: "Don't move. Don't move a muscle. Jim. Listen to me. Jim. There's a little boy in the corner of your room right now. Far corner. By the window, in the shadows. He has no head, Jim. He doesn't have a head. And he wants to hurt you."

The words came in crystal clear as if I was wearing an earpiece.

What the hell was happening? Was this real? Was I projecting it, scaring myself with an overactive imagination that *wants* to hear something, so my mind invented it?

I froze. I kept my eyes shut. Afraid to look.

Chills ran over my body like rain, like crawling fingers, bugs, like flurries of static.

I felt my stomach drop, I felt my heart rate increase. Anxiety.

Why am I so terrified? This is NONSENSE!

By the window, in the shadows.

He has no head, Jim. He doesn't have a head. And he wants to hurt you.

If I rolled over, I'd be facing that exact corner where the voice told me the headless little boy was, but my gut said not to do it.

I sensed something in the room, like I was being watched. I felt anxiety building.

My heart pounded. My ears throbbed. I felt lightheaded. Dizzy. The throb in my head came back. My neck tense, taut. I could feel the tendons tight like wire, ready.

Fight or flight kicking in.

My eyes were wide.

It seemed somehow darker in the room. The darkness seemed different. Usually light from the streets coming in from the window and from the TV downstairs cast a glow on the room, but not tonight.

Tonight the darkness was thick. Blinding. Like a shadow over the entire room, painting the walls and air pitch black.

I felt like I had when I was a kid, when I used to be afraid in my room at night. Paralyzed with terror. Every noise sounded larger, bigger. Close up.

He has no head, Jim. He doesn't have a head. And he wants to hurt you.

I also couldn't help but think this was ridiculous, and that I could prove this whole thing was just my imagination if I simply looked in the corner and saw what was there waiting for me: Nothing.

Probably nothing.

Yet I couldn't turn around. I was afraid I'd instead see exactly what the voice said would be there.

Am I losing my mind?

"He's reaching his hands out to you now," the voice warned me, clearer than ever. "Don't move. Don't breathe.

One move and you'll set him off, and he will take your head."

The voice was a whisper, a sliver through the black of the room, like a hiss, sinister.

My heart was thrashing in my ears, and I felt feverish and sick. Why was I so terrified? I remembered back to so many sleepless nights as a kid in my bedroom at my parent's house, eyes crammed shut, focusing on every sound, every feeling of horror and dread—too terrified to even call out for my dad.

I thought I heard something shift behind me in the dark. From the corner.

I felt the rush of adrenaline hit me and in one sudden movement, surprising myself even, I rolled over and sat up in bed, my eyes fixed and focused on the corner of the room the voice warned me about.

The corner was about five feet away from the bed. Shadows, pitch black. I let my eyes sit and adjust. I leaned in slightly.

The outline of a boy, perhaps eight or nine.

Arms out but not moving. Motionless. My feet and hands went numb and tingly, as if asleep.

The shadow of the boy had no head.

It's my imagination...

"Hi, Jim."

Not in my head.

The voice was in the room. In the corner.

And what I was seeing was real. It was a boy, with no head—reaching out to me—like the voice in my head warned me about.

He wants to hurt you.

Reaching out to me, straining—like he was begging for help or waiting for a hug or desperately wanting to be picked up. He was grasping in the dark to find something to cling onto and not let go. I could see the small fingers on his hands reaching, grasping, clenching, and unclenching. Searching.

Suddenly a weight on the bed next to me, in Sarah's spot, the feeling of a small hand on my shoulder and breath in my ear and the whisper of a child: "...let me introduce you to my friend."

The room was buzzing. Alarms going off in my head. I tore out of bed, panic-stricken and ran to the light switch, looking over my shoulder, eyes glued toward the corner of the bedroom and my bed while I frantically smacked the wall until I found the switch to flick it on. The little boy was still there. Flicked the switch.

Light stung my eyes like white lightning, dizzy and disorienting as the room came into focus.

Empty.

The corner by the window was just the corner by the window. The bed, the blankets were ruffled only where I had been. No trace of anything.

The hum of the furnace. The ticking of the blinds on the windows. The snow gently falling outside.

My heart racing and banging in my ears.

And then right next to me: "Jim?"

I jumped and shouted.

It was Sarah. She laughed.

"You okay? I heard something, it sounded like you were banging on the walls in here. Did something happen?"

"Jesus Christ, you scared me," I said, letting out a relieved laugh. I eyeballed the room again, shaken.

"What happened?" she asked, a confused smile. She could sense I was not myself.

My mind was a blur of panic and worry. Was I losing my mind? Did that just happen?

I hadn't been this afraid since I was a kid.

I just fucking saw a little boy with no head. In my room. I heard it. I felt something.

"Honestly," I lied, my adrenaline pumping, "I thought I heard something. I thought it might be a mouse or something shuffling around. I freaked out. But it was just the furnace vent blowing the blinds around. I'm being jittery and stupid. You know how I hate mice."

My voice was shaking, breathing erratic, like I'd been running.

"Sounded like a brawl going on," she said, chuckling. Slight concern flickered in her eyes.

"Sorry if I scared you," I smiled. "I think I just scared myself."

"We don't have mice. And if we do – another reason why we should get a cat."

I exhaled, smiling, trying to sound relaxed. "We aren't getting a stupid cat."

She winked, "Well, get some sleep, scaredy cat. I'm gonna go back downstairs for a bit. Oh, and I scared *you*? You scared *me*! Sounded like a bunch of wild animals trampling around up here!"

She kissed me on the cheek and went back downstairs. I stayed standing by the light switch, still slightly trembling, staring at the corner by the bed. I felt like a kid again, afraid of the dark.

What the hell just happened?

"What did you say?" Sarah called from downstairs.

Did I say that out loud?

"Sorry! Nothing! Just said good night!"

As I crawled into bed, I turned the night table lamp on. It was going to stay on. Childish of me, I know, but when I was a kid it was the only thing that would let me get to sleep. If I could see the room, I'd be fine. It was the dark that used to frighten me. The light distracted me from the dark, from my own imagination. From the voices in my head.

My imagination had always been active, and now I had worked myself up.

The light stayed on.

Sarah would simply think I fell asleep with the lamp on. She wouldn't even think anything of it.

The hum of the furnace. The ticking of the blinds. No voices.

Sleep.

———

I awoke to the sound of Sarah screaming. Kind of a scream. It was a far more terrifying sound.

She was screaming as much as one can while sleeping, her lungs trying to force out as much air as possible, her body paralyzed by the grip of deep sleep.

She was making muffled whimpering sounds – like she was being strangled by pure terror.

I froze for a split second before realizing what was happening. I quickly sat up and shook Sarah awake.

She flailed her arms, jarred out of sleep, confused. Eyes wide and immediately calmed.

"Sarah?" I asked.

She looked at me in the dark, quiet. An odd expression on her face.

When she replied, her voice had a calmer tone. No longer remotely terrified.

"I just had the dumbest dream..."

It sounded like she was about to tell me what the dream was and decided not to, mid-sentence.

"What? Nightmare?" I thought of the voice, the boy.

"No...kinda. It was stupid. I don't even wanna say. Dumb dream. I'm fine. I'll go back to sleep."

"Well, now you have to tell me!" I half laughed, but I also felt my heart picking up its pace.

"Honestly," she said, laying back down and rolling over. "It was stupid. A dumb dream and it startled me more than anything. I don't even wanna talk about it. Was stupid. G'night."

I let my eyes adjust, staring at the ceiling. What the heck could her dream have been about that she didn't want to say? The dumbest dream? It was stupid? Why did she scream, then?

And if it was so stupid – why couldn't she tell me?

I briefly thought of the boy with no head. Perhaps it was all as real as the sound of the door slamming shut: Just a dream.

———

The 7 a.m. alarm went off as usual. However, this morning was strange because Sarah was already out of bed. I could smell coffee and faintly hear the radio playing downstairs.

I found her on the couch reading.

"Morning," she said without looking up from her phone.

"You're up early." I grabbed a cup and poured myself a coffee.

"Woke up and couldn't fall back to sleep," she said.

"You had that nightmare last night."

She laughed. "Oh yeah. So dumb."

In the light of the morning it felt safer to ask her about it.

"You said it was dumb last night too. What was it about?"

She looked at me strangely and smiled, as if dismissing.

"Honestly, I didn't want to freak you out. It was super stupid though." She paused.

"I had this dream, we were in a bedroom just like ours, but it was a bit bigger, the walls were a different colour. It was actually kind of nice. You were there and your back was to me, and I got the sense you were mad. I called your name, and you turned around and you had no face." She laughed then, shaking her head and continued.

"Like I said, it was the dumbest thing. It was like you just had a dark hole where your face should have been. But then from the dark hole you started screaming. And it sounded like this high pitched, tortured, angry wail! So loud! I literally screamed and I guess I screamed in real life too and woke you up and then you woke me. Freaky dream. But stupid."

I wasn't entirely sure if "stupid" was the right word. It was creepy as hell.

I thought of the little boy that I thought I saw.

He wants to hurt you. If he senses you, he'll take your head.

My ears buzzed and I felt panic rising in my chest.

I brushed the thought away because I was freaking myself out again.

And that's all any of this was: Just me freaking myself out. Again.

———

Hell bent on freaking myself out, later that night I found myself on my phone doing some more reading about voices and clairaudience and visions. I felt like I was doing all of this on the sly, without Sarah knowing. She'd think I was crazy.

You can go down the rabbit hole of nonsense when you start digging in and it's hard to tell if any of it is real or if it's all just a big mess of people with overactive imaginations.

The content I was reading was wild and very unbelievable. I couldn't help but ask myself: Is it someone's actual experience? Or someone's work of fiction?

Truly, it was hard to tell if any of what happened to me was real or my own imagination.

I was flipping through various testimonials from people claiming to have had encounters with ghosts, spirits, the dead and other supernatural phenomena when I chanced upon a familiar face. It took me a second to place her, but when I did, I couldn't believe the coincidence.

Peggy Watts. Clairvoyant, clairaudient, medium, psychic. The same psychic I saw on that talk show so many years ago.

Of course, she was a bit older, but seeing as it had to have been at least 25 years since I saw her on that show, she didn't look *that* much different.

The heavy tan, the bleached hair, the chunky gold jewellery–it was still there. There was a tug of war going on between her aging face and some plastic surgery, but other than that, she looked pretty much the same as I remembered her.

I clicked on her social media, and it was extremely active. She'd been busy. More books, countless appearances on TV, radio, a YouTube channel with weekly episodes in which she did readings and gave advice to fans and followers.

Her words on that talk show always stuck with me. She nailed what it was like to hear the voices and even just glancing through her extensive body of work and research, I figured she might have more information–a book–anything, on what I could possibly be experiencing. Answers. Something.

To say she had been busy was an understatement.

She must have upwards of fifty books now, with some pretty out there titles: *Astral Projection: Your Passport to Worlds Unimaginable!, Shadows from The Void, Nightmares and Sleep Scares, Learning to Listen to your Intuition, Signs from the Afterlife.* The typical books written by so-called psychics usually found on the shelves of new age book stores and shops that sell crystals and incense.

She had a large following; her website even listed her as assisting police in solving crimes.

I continued scrolling through her book titles. I couldn't tell what would be helpful, and I really had no clue if any of it was anything more than straight up nonsense.

That's the thing about psychics. Who knows if they are real? But scams? Scams are absolutely a thing.

She might just be some crazy dingbat who knows how to talk persuasively and can write and market herself. Half these supposed "psychics" are simply people with a talent for pushing other people's buttons. All it takes is the right tone and wording and if it all equals out to *exactly* what desperate people want to hear, you got it made.

Really, she's writing about things that *no one* has any real answer to.

Yet, here I was. Searching. And scam or not – she seemed to know a thing or two about exactly what I was experiencing. So, what else did she have to say on the subject?

One title jumped out at me. *Dead Air: Tuning into the Voices - A Guide to Clairaudience.*

This was the one. As I debated whether to order the book right there or make a note to look for it at the local bookstore, I saw something even more interesting: The "Contact Peggy" button.

I did notice on her social media she seemed to be very interactive and responsive to people who reached out. Who knows if it was actually the "real" her or some social media or PR manager answering for her, but by the look of some of her online back-and-forth, it appeared to actually be Peggy Watts.

I clicked the button and fired off a fast message to her, feeling a bit silly. Part of me felt like I was writing a fan letter, another part of me wondered if I was going a bit too far.

But why not?

. . .

Hi Peggy,

I saw you years back on a talk show and you were talking to a little boy in the audience who could hear voices. You compared the voices to hearing a radio playing in the other room. It really spoke to me because I experience the same thing. Lately I've been experiencing it a bit more intensely. I feel a bit silly writing to you, but I am curious if in your research and experience with people, if anyone ever had the voices speak directly to them, and if they ever saw anything. I had a strange experience the other night and thought I saw a small child in my room. The voices told me the child wanted to hurt me. Again, I know this sounds crazy and you probably get bombarded with messages like this, but if you have a good book or any advice to point me in the right direction, I'm very interested in learning more about what's going on.

Thanks for your time,
Jim

I glanced at Sarah who was over on the other couch reading news. She had no idea I just emailed a famous talk show psychic. I could only imagine the eye roll if she did. And perhaps rightfully so. Who knew if Peggy Watts would even get back to me? Even her name sounded totally made up.

Still, last night was something. Could it have been a dream? Was I losing my mind? Could be. Who knows?

———

Sarah came to bed that night earlier than usual, which was nice, but it also made every sound in the house a bit of a mystery. Usually, when I'm up there alone and she's downstairs, any noises I hear I can blame on her moving around, or the TV.

The house felt empty below us as we curled up on our own sides of the bed after saying our goodnights.

I listened.

It's funny how all houses make noises. No matter what kind of shape they're in. New builds will settle. Older houses creak and crack for no reason. You get used to it. It's like the house is breathing or settling in for the night as well. Like saying goodnight. A fine line between comforting and creepy.

I listened harder. I could faintly hear the fridge humming downstairs.

I tried to focus on it, isolate it the way the website said to.

I heard a small crack on the stairs. *Just the house settling.*

A car drove by in that same lonely whoosh, the headlights reflecting off the wall for a moment before gliding away with the sound of the car disappearing down the street. When I was a kid, I used to think the light reflected on the walls from passing cars looked like faces, like spirits floating by, checking in.

There was a heavy, thick silence in the house. I wondered if Sarah was asleep.

Her breathing was a slow, rhythmic, relaxed pace. Probably getting there.

I decided to try again and call out to ...it. Whatever it was. The voice. Invite it in to talk.

Hey this is Jim. I'm here. If you're real, tell me what you want. I'm here. Let's talk.

Almost immediately, a response:

...Jim...

I felt my ears grow hot. My body tingled with electricity, a buzz. Pins and needles, we called it when we were kids.

For the sake of momentum I kept it going: *Who are you?*

You know who I am Jim...when you gonna introduce me to your friend?

More chills tingling all over my body.

Who are you? I repeated in my head.

The voice responded: *Countdown is on Jim...*

What countd–I began to ask, but it interrupted me, and the voice began rapidly counting down:

10, 9, 8, 7, 6, 5, 4, 3, 2... and the voice paused.

I could hear my heart pounding. Something in the corner of the room made a small snapping noise. I jumped slightly. Silence.

I thought I heard someone breathing heavily near the closet.

I froze.

NOW! The voice BOOMED in my ears, and Sarah bolted up screaming, arms flailing as if she was trying to fight someone off: Me. She was hitting me, slapping me frantically.

"Sarah! Sarah! Sarah, wake up! It's a dream! Sarah! Wake up!!"

I held her arms away from me as she swiped in the air, hitting my chest and head. She resisted, terrified and struggling against me. Then she stopped and looked around in the dark, breathing fast, as if she'd been running.

"Oh my god, Jim? Where is he?" She was frantic, tense, almost in a dazed, manic state as she became more awake. "Jim! Jim, turn the light on. TURN THE LIGHT ON!" Her voice was shrill, screaming in emergency mode.

I jumped out of bed and hit the switch. Sarah was sitting up, blankets clutched to her chest defensively, eyes darting around the room, heaving breaths, nearly hyper-ventilating. She looked absolutely terrified.

"Sarah? Sarah. What? What's wrong?!" I felt my own breath increasing, heart rate pounding.

"Did you see it? Did you see him?" she asked. Her eyes

were wild, pupils dilated. I could barely recognize her. She was in such a state of panic.

"See what!?" I tried to keep a calm voice, but I was shaking. "Sarah, you were having a dream."

She paused, as if processing it, thinking about what she just experienced. A confused look on her face, as if she couldn't believe it could have possibly been a dream. She seemed completely disoriented. She was sweating, still breathing heavily.

"Sarah. You're okay. It was a nightmare." I tried to use the gentlest, most soothing voice I could conjure up.

It happened right at the end of that countdown. And then there was the snap in the corner of the room. And the breathing.

And Sarah freaked.

I tried to remain calm, and I focused on Sarah.

"Sarah? You're okay. Right? You are, okay? It was a dream, Sarah."

Her breathing began to return to normal and finally she spoke.

"I guess it was a dream, but it seemed so real." She swallowed and cleared her voice, her eyes still scanning the room with dread and suspicion.

"There was a guy hiding in the corner of the room." Her eyes shot to the corner. The same corner I saw the little boy – or whatever it was– I thought I saw the night before.

"He was crouched down. I could make him out perfectly. His shape. I couldn't see his face, but it was a guy. I was frozen because I couldn't believe what I was seeing. I was paralyzed. I couldn't even scream. And the guy was shaped weird. And he started creeping closer and closer to the bed and he got right up in your face and started screaming words in some weird language. Loud. He sounded like a demon or something. And that's what I was doing, I was trying to fight him off you. And I guess I woke up. But Jim, it was so real."

Chills ran through my body and I felt dizzy, feverish. I hugged her.

"And for a split second, when you were waking me up, I couldn't see your face. It was just all shadows, so I thought it was him."

She was truly shaken.

It felt like ice shards were sliding down my body. *What the hell was happening?*

"Sarah, it was a total dream. No creepy man here, unless you count me," I tried to joke.

She smiled. Finally, a sign she was okay.

"Can I get you anything? A glass of water? Did you want to get up and watch TV? Something light to clear your head?"

"I'm okay. I'm probably over-tired. I'm good. I'm gonna go back to sleep."

She still sounded shaky, but better.

"You sure?"

"Honestly, I'm good. I just wanna go back to sleep. I'm good."

I stared at her for a moment as she fluffed her pillow and laid back down and then I got up and flicked the light back off and crawled into bed.

"Jim?" she asked in the dark.

"Yeah?"

"Care if we leave the lamp on? Just as a nightlight? It's stupid I know..."

I reached for my phone and turned the lamp on with the app.

"Love you, Jim," she said.

"Love you too."

As I was putting my phone back on the charger, I noticed a notification of a new email.

That was quick:

Peggy Watts got back to me. The message she left had me wondering if I was in over my head or if I truly was losing it.

———

I barely slept. The next morning I was staring at Peggy's email, debating what to do.

Peggy Watts' message was short and to the point, and I couldn't help but read it in her hoarse, no-bullshit voice when I went over it again and again.

Hi Jim,

Thanks for reaching out. This is tough to speak on through an email.

Some general advice, and again I don't know your situation, but be careful how you acknowledge these voices. You very well could be picking up some transmissions from a place I call "The Void," which I often reference in my books.

It's okay to listen to them, most of what they say is nonsense. But they will reach out directly to you if they see you as an "in" because they are looking for a way out of The Void. Don't let them in.

Don't invite them in.

It's okay to listen. But you're in dangerous territory when you start talking back to them, especially if you don't know who they are.

If you want to speak to me in person, I do one-on-one sessions. The fees are on my website and you can book a time slot.

I also recommend my book *Transmissions from The Void*, which is specific to what you are experiencing.

All my best,

PW

Figures. So, I get a pitch to call her 1-800 number and a plug for her book.

Now what?

I did a quick search for her *Transmissions from The Void* book. Zero copies in stock.

Of course.

Browsing through her website a bit deeper and looking at the different options and packages she had, I came to realize that a session with Peggy Watts was not cheap.

Two hundred and fifty dollars for a half hour.

That was the lowest price point I could find. It included a Facetime chat, and I could ask whatever questions I wanted.

Two hundred and fifty dollars.

It was a lot of money but not an insane amount either. I'd spent more on concerts, and shopping trips.

I couldn't deny what I'd heard and seen. I couldn't deny what I was experiencing or what might have been trickling over to Sarah.

When you gonna introduce me to your friend?

What if this was actually real, as Peggy Watts stated, and I was wading through "dangerous territory?"

I shook my head as I found myself clicking on the "book now" link and reached for my wallet to grab my credit card. I made a silent plea to the universe that I wasn't flushing a quarter of my cheque down the toilet to someone who very well could have the credibility of a fortune cookie.

———

I opened my laptop and logged in with all the coordinates I received via email from Peggy's "team" after booking with her yesterday.

It was mid-afternoon, dazzling bright light from the snowy mid-day sun shining through the window.

An eerie calm settling in.

Sarah wasn't home from work yet and wouldn't be for a few hours.

It was for the best. I didn't tell her I was doing this. A whirlwind was going through my head while I waited to connect with Peggy.

What was I doing? Was I crazy? What kind of danger could I be in? Is there a way to stop hearing these voices? Was I being taken for a $250 ride and giving away a half hour of my life I'll never get back to some quack?

Valid question, but I probably wouldn't ask Peggy that.

My screen flickered and lit up–a camera being turned on. A bright light, the lens and contrast adjusted, and Peggy Watts came into view.

I was a bit star struck. I had been reading up about her, reading bits of her books that were published online, watching old TV show clips. I mean, I knew of this woman since I was a kid and here she was about to have a one-on-one chat with me.

She looked a bit older than her website showed. Less makeup. Less fancy lighting.

Honey brown hair, considerable amount of eyeliner, tanned skin that saw years of sun-bathing and gold lipstick. Lots of beads and crystals around her neck and bracelets around her wrist. Exactly what you'd expect. As seen on TV.

From what I could see it looked like she was broadcasting out of an office. Nothing special. A brown bookshelf behind her and some kind of cloth wall hanging with what looked like cycles of the moon on it.

"Hello," she said in her raspy, cigarette-stained voice. "This is Jim? Can you hear me, Jim?"

"Hi!" I said, sounding a bit too enthusiastic and like a fan. I toned it down ever so slightly.

"This is Jim. I can hear you."

"Hi honey. Alright so I'm recording all of this, and I'll send you a copy to your email as soon as we finish. You can ask any questions you want. You're the one who I was emailing with so we are already ahead of the game on that. Just a quick rundown, sweetie. I'm going to start the timer and I'm going to give you some of my thoughts just based on what you wrote in your email and in your consultation request and then I'll open it up to your questions. Sound good, hon?"

She had a warmth about her. Straight forward. I got the impression she didn't need to be here. She was just doing this because this is what she does. Not a whole lot of bells and whistles, just cutting right to it.

I nodded.

"Okay I'm going to hit the record button and we can get started."

She pushed a button on her screen, her image flickered and stabilized, and she began.

"Alright Jim, I'm approaching this conversation assuming you are of sound mental health. People with mental illness, schizophrenia and such, they often hear voices. I'm going to assume you are not mentally ill, but if you are unsure you have to speak to someone else and it's not a psychic, okay? I'm not your girl if that's the case, and I can't help you with mental illness. You need someone who went to school and knows the science of the brain and psychiatry for that. But what you say you are experiencing is something I have heard over and over. You're hearing voices as if they are coming in. Like a radio broadcast. One you can barely hear. That's what I call a transmission from The Void. Now I don't know what The Void is, that's just what I call it. I only know it's not *here*. It's somewhere *else*. It's filled with good and bad, and they are constantly broadcasting out messages. Most of us here don't pick up on it. But some of *us*, people like you and I, do. Some of us have an antenna in our heads that picks up these messages and we can listen in. And that's mostly what it is. Listening in. You're overhearing a conversation in progress, and it probably doesn't make sense. Most people pay no mind and dismiss it. Others can home in and hear it more clearly. Now I'm not asking you to believe any of this, okay sweetie, I'm just telling you what I believe to be true because you paid me to do exactly that."

She paused as if waiting for me to respond.

"Okay," I said. Everything she was saying was nothing I hadn't heard her say before on talk shows, even the talk show I saw as a kid.

"Okay. So before we go any further I have to ask you, Jim. Did you speak back to these voices or invite them in, in any way? Did you acknowledge the voices in any way at all that could even be interpreted as inviting them in?"

I told her about some of the websites I'd been looking at, how I'd been reading up on clairaudience and the instructions on how to develop it. I admitted I had called out into the beyond, as the site suggested and how the messages became more direct and then things started to happen.

Hesitating, I confessed that I was pretty sure I actually used the word "invite" when talking to this voice.

"NO, no, no!!" she said, slapping the palm of her hand down on her desk.

She actually looked angry. And exhausted, like she'd dealt with this before and was sick and tired of it.

"This is exactly why, Jim, we don't invite them in! This is exactly why! Half of those sites have no idea what they're talking about, and they're reckless with the information they give out. Here's the thing, Jim, half the people who believe they hear voices are sick. The other half *want* to hear the voices, but don't have the antenna in their head. There are a small few who have a perfectly good antenna, and they pick up messages. The transmissions from The Void are looking for antennas. That's their way in. You gave them a way in, and they're going to try to force their way through even more. More power, more influence. They're going to be harder to ignore. The more you acknowledge them, the more influence they have over here."

She wasn't selling anything. Well, she was, but I already bought it so that was irrelevant. She seemed genuinely concerned. I told her about the dreams. About Sarah. About the little boy with no head. About the sounds. About what I saw in my bedroom. She wasn't remotely phased by it, but she seemed to express general worry about my wellbeing. And Sarah's.

She slanted her eyes at me almost suspiciously. As if she knew something.

"This is not your first run-in with these voices, is it? You have spoken to them before. Is this true?"

I laughed for a minute. It was a nervous laugh that came out when I truly had no idea how to respond to someone. I wasn't sure what she was talking about and then she said:

"When you were a kid, hon. This would have been when you were a kid. That's what I'm picking up. Were you ever really sick?"

Back when I was a kid. I let my mind travel back to *that* time. Something I didn't like to do. I didn't like to swim through those memories. At least not too deep into them.

Yes. When I was a kid I was home sick quite a bit. I had what the doctors called viral pneumonia, but even they weren't fully sure what it was.

I started to tell her about that time in my life. Something I hadn't thought about for decades.

But now, thinking back: It all made sense about what was happening today.

———

Thirty Years Prior

I'm six years old and I'm in my bed. Except it doesn't feel like it. I hear bees buzzing in my ears and I keep swatting them away. I can hear my heartbeat like it's inside my head. I'm sweating but I'm cold. I can see the light from the hallway, and it looks so far away even though I know it's right there. Why does my doorway look so far away?

The bees get louder in my ears, and I hear voices.

My body aches.

I can see the silhouettes of my toys on my shelf and suddenly it's as if I am inches away from them. The faces of my stuffed animals and figurines smiling at me. They look scary.

Suddenly my face is so close to the ceiling it's like my nose is about to bump the light fixture that hangs above my bed.

But my body can feel my mattress. The weight of the blankets is heavy on me, but it's like I'm floating above my bed. Colours are swirling in the dark. The buzzing is getting louder.

I can hear walking on my bedroom carpet, but I can't see anyone.

Swish, swish, swish. What is happening?

I'm spinning. I start coughing. I'm going to be sick. I'm scared.

Now my face is pressed against the far corner, higher than I've ever been before in my bedroom. Am I flying? Why am I so scared? I feel like I'm in bed, but when I open my eyes, it's like the dimensions of my room keep changing. Nothing makes sense. I feel gigantic and I feel tiny.

I call out to my father, and I am back in my bed, the bees still roaring in my ears.

I see my father's shape come into the room. He doesn't turn the light on.

"You okay, Jimmy?" he asks.

"I need a glass of water."

"I'll get you some," he says. I start coughing as I hear him walk away.

But something is wrong. Something is not right.

He left my room, but his shadow—his shape–remains in my room.

Standing. Staring. Motionless.

Yet, I can hear him, his slippers on the hallway carpet leaving my room. His feet hitting the smooth tile of the kitchen. Rummaging for a plastic cup in the pantry. Turning on the faucet in the sink. The cup filling.

I hear all of this, but his shadow remains in my bedroom, over my bed, staring at me.

It looks just like my dad, but I know it's not my dad.

And there is something else I know, but I don't know how I know it: This thing that looks like my dad wants to hurt me. I am scared of it, and I don't know why. I have to pee.

I can hear the buzzing in my ears getting louder. And I hear whispers, behind the buzzing.

Right in my ear. I can practically feel the breath of whoever is speaking, hot on my skin, but I can't tell who it is. The shadow remains still. It seems to have gotten bigger.

"...he wants your head, Jimmy..."

The shape of the thing that kind of looks like my dad moves ever so slightly towards me and begins to slowly crouch down. I still can't make out any details.

"...give him your head, Jimmy..."

Its voice sounds like an angry whisper.

Whatever is in my room is now completely crouched by my bed. Face to face with me. Except I can't see a face. It's just shadow. This close, I should at least be able to see some detail.

I hear my father rummaging in the kitchen, and I look back to the shape in front of me.

I lean in closer.

"Dad?" I whisper.

Bright red eyes appear in the dark, the buzzing becomes deafening and the voice in my ears screams so loudly the pain causes me to cry out.

"GIVE HIM YOUR HEAD!" the voice shouts.

Suddenly my dad is switching the light on and handing me a cup of water. I am crying. He feels my forehead. I am burning up. I peed in my PJS.

The buzzing is still there but quieter. The shape, the image of whatever that was in my room, is gone, disappeared when the light turned on. My real dad is here and the other thing is gone.

I tell my father what I saw and what I heard. I'm crying and shaking.

"It's the fever, you have nightmares when you have a fever," he touches my forehead and looks worried. "You're getting really sick."

My parents let me sleep in their bed that night. I feel better and safe with them on either side of me.

As I drift off to sleep, I see the image of the thing in my room again, now in their room. In the corner. I stare. The buzzing begins.

"I'll be right here, Jimmy," it whispers as if in my ears. Crystal clear. Loud.

"Gimme, gimme, gimme..."

Chills trace down my spine and sweat pours off my body.

It's just the fever, it's just the fever, it's just the fever, I say to myself over and over.

I lay frozen all night long, staring at the shape, and it staring back at me, poised as if ready to pounce. Only darkness where its face should be. The entire room feels like it's quilted in a shadow. I've never felt so afraid, like I'm going to die.

———

It was a long time ago.

I told Peggy how I had viral pneumonia, how I heard voices. I hallucinated. I felt afraid.

That winter, when I was six, the whites of my eyes turned red because all the blood vessels broke with the force of my coughing. I was afraid to look in a mirror because it looked like my eyes were bleeding.

My parents must have been terrified. More terrified than they let on.

They covered all the mirrors in the house so I wouldn't have to see my scary, sick reflection glaring back at me with bloody eyes.

Today when they talk about it, they refer to it as "the time you almost died."

My sickness started the night the room went all funny. The night I saw that thing that was imitating my dad.

That's also when I started to hear the transmissions from The Void.

I didn't think much about that time in my life or that thing that I saw. But I knew now, clear as day, the thing that was in my room that night was somehow the same thing that is tuned into me now.

It waited. It called out to me all through the years.

And finally, I invited it back in.

"And that's another way they get you," Peggy Watts said.

"When you're weak. That's a way in. In your case, back then, you were young. A lot was happening to you that you didn't understand. Very easy to brush away what you were seeing as a hallucination from the fever. And that's how it was explained to you. And because you were a child, that's how you understood it. But it was something else. And sweetie when that shape told you they would be waiting, they didn't lie. This is them coming back for you. The boy with no head. The man. The shape. The menacing. The shadows, the dreams. This all makes sense!"

She slapped the palm of her hand down on her desk again and the crystals on her bracelet jingled.

This was happening. That thing I saw in my room, the shadow I'd catch glimpses of now and then as I grew up...it was real. Just like I *knew* that it was real when I was a kid.

I had dismissed them as fever dreams, or sickness-induced nightmares.

Dismissed.

"Dismissed," Peggy said. "Because you didn't know what you were dealing with. You weren't tuning in to them, so you weren't giving them any power. You weren't inviting them in. Your illness explained it away, and you accepted that because you didn't know what it was that was trying to get at you. Now you know. So, you need to take some steps. You've already invited them in so you're more at risk now."

"What steps?" I asked. "What? Sage the bedroom? A circle of salt around my bed? Call in an exorcist?" She shook her head and gestured with her hand as if to wave away everything I said as nonsense.

"No, it's not that complicated. Here's the thing. You are an antenna. If you honed your skills, you could be sitting where I'm sitting making all kinds of money doing what I'm doing with you right now.

"But you can't because they found a way in and now as

long as you are picking up and receiving what they are sending to you, that's an open door for them. And let me tell you, they will not stop trying to barge into that door for as long as it's open. So sweetie let me tell you what you have to do, it'll only work if you listen and do it. But it will work."

She paused. "First rule, sweetie–and this is the tricky part about these things–they are only as real as we make them."

———

I nearly lost my mind when I was a kid. At least, I thought at the time I was losing my mind. I thought I was legitimately losing my head, and the same thoughts were going through my brain now.

I spoke with Peggy Watts for another 45 minutes, well over my paid-for time slot.

So much of what she told me washed over me, and I'd need to listen to the recording of our session many times to fully understand.

But for now, I had some demons to get rid of.

She told me these things—these voices from The Void— are mostly harmless. She described them as guides with bits of information they can pass on to us.

Some are harder to hear than others, but nothing they can say will hurt anyone.

But there are a few who try to influence the receptor– that's me–and use them for whatever plan they have. She wasn't sure what it was. Drive me to insanity? Create a cloud of negativity? Push me or Sarah over the edge until something drastic happens? It could be anything, but it wasn't good.

She told me I was right that these things wanted to cause me harm. To what extent, she couldn't say.

But the more I tune in, the stronger they will get.

"They come for you in those moments when sleep and

being awake are fusing together. Your guard will be down. Be careful. They are coming for you. Your first mistake was inviting them in. Don't feed them."

————

That's what I kept thinking in bed that night.

"Don't feed them."

I knew what to do but had no idea how it would work, or if I'd be able to do it.

It was snowing heavily. Thick, chunky flakes coming down. It was the kind of snow that was going to accumulate. Pile up. Insulate.

Snow muffles the world. It makes the noises we hear sound less harsh. It buries everything in mounds of soft ice.

There is something to be said about a wintery night: It can be both bleak and comforting at the same time.

Tonight, I was hoping the snow would be a blanket, a cover, a comfort.

"Jim."

A man's voice. Calm. Firm. Strong. I listened.

Quiet. The snow blowing outside.

And then:

"Jimmy?"

Sarah's voice. Sounding worried. She never called me Jimmy.

And that was my first clue that it wasn't really Sarah.

I could hear her downstairs, but it sounded like she was right in the room, in the doorway, calling my name.

This was it.

"Jim," an unrecognizable voice said, impatiently. "Turn around Jim. Look at me."

Don't feed them, I thought to myself. *Don't feed them,*

don't feed them don't feed them don't feed th–I inhaled sharply and held it. And I saw it.

There was a man crouched beside my dresser six feet away from me. Crouched down, like an intruder, hiding and even though I couldn't see his face, I knew he was staring at me in the dark.

I don't know if he knew that I could see him, not sure if he knew I knew he was there, so I stayed motionless and watched him.

His profile was sinister, his shadow sat, lurking, waiting.

I could hear a small hum building. A buzzing.

I sensed him moving. Crouching lower, like a cat about to pounce.

I kept my eyes fixed on him, but I could see out the window next to him that the snow continued to pound down outside, billowing, blowing. I could see it drifting and piling on the streets.

Insulate. Muffle. Bury.

The thing, the man, began to creep towards the bed, the shadow. Arms freakishly long. Proportions off.

The buzzing getting louder. I could hear it shuffling slowly toward me.

This was real. This was not a dream. This was happening.

Except it wasn't.

"First rule, sweetie–here's the thing about these things–they are only as real as we make them."

I closed my eyes calmly, despite every instinct telling me to get up, scream and run for safety. I shut my eyes gently and tried to envision white noise. Static. Dead air to drown them away. Snow to bury away the sound. I thought of the snow. Tried to focus on hearing the snow come down.

That was the key. Find something else to drown them out. Focus on that sound. Find your peace in it.

That's what Peggy Watts had instructed me to do.

Simple enough, but easier said than done.

"It'll get easier, hun. There is a hole in you that they want to come through. Plug it. Tune it out. Focus on other things. Ignore. Dismiss it. It's just noise. Don't give it any power."

I kept my eyes closed.

I'm just a guy in bed. I'm just a guy in bed. I'm just a guy in bed.

And then I heard it whisper:

"I'm right here, Jim."

I focused on my breathing. Kept my eyes closed. White noise. Quiet. Calm.

I was trying to not let my heart beat out of my chest, to slow it down. I felt a cough coming on. I felt the cold burn of a fever shiver over my body. I knew if I opened my eyes, the thing would be inches from my face and I'd lose it.

I'd lose my head.

So I kept my eyes closed. I kept breathing. I could sense it. I could hear the buzzing grow louder. It was terrifying. Tense. Erratic. Amplified.

They are only as real as we make them.

My thoughts turned to my childhood. Mountains of snow, my dad shovelling the sidewalks and me helping with my small plastic scoop.

The surprising warmth of the walls of the snow fort my father built for me.

The blinding neon light of the sun reflecting off the crusted snow, sparkling.

The way the wind would blow, creating snow drifts. I focused on the sound of the wind and the way it melted everything away. In real life and tonight, in my head.

The sound of the snow coming down suffocated out the buzzing. I focused. I tuned in to the static as the rest fell away.

Snow softens. Smothers. Stifles.

In this case, the smooth static sound I was focusing on was going to asphyxiate whatever it was that was after me.

I would not tune in. My antenna would only pick up static. Snow would block the signal.

And as the snow continued to pile up and wrap our neighbourhood in sparkling white flakes, I could feel the thing retreating into the shadows, and further.

Sleep took me.

I awoke in the night and Sarah was sleeping soundly beside me.

The room was bright from the moon reflecting off the white layers of snow in the neighbourhood.

We were warm in bed. I heard the buzz start up again, but I closed my eyes, smiling – and focused on the sound of the snow.

We slept through the night.

———

The same way I broke my radio antenna as a kid when I accidentally dropped my boom box, I disabled the antenna that picked up transmissions from The Void.

"Focusing on nothing and clearing your mind is a tricky thing to do," Peggy Watts had told me.

That night in my bedroom I thought of snow to muffle it all away. Plugging up the hole.

Safety.

Just like anxiety, the more you feed it the worse it gets. Sometimes a simple focus on breathing, heart-rate and a whole lot of calm and comfort helps ease the sting of fear and paranoia.

A simple concentrated effort to stay present and focus on what's real is easier said than done.

Peggy Watts mentioned a white noise generator as a tool I

could use to help drown out the other noises. And it helped. I turned it on every night and I focused on the waves of static it sent out.

Not only did it drown out the voices at night, it was a sleep aid too.

And this is how it would be. Because this is how it was.

My head was an antenna. When I was a child something bad found a way to connect to it and broadcast directly to me.

If I couldn't hear it, it couldn't hurt me. If I didn't acknowledge it, it couldn't get me.

That's a tough thing to remember when you see a shadow in the corner of your room, creeping up on you.

It's difficult to stay calm when you hear voices telling you that something wants to hurt you.

It's near impossible to stay sane when you see the image of a child with no head, arms outstretched and fingers wiggling, searching, grasping.

Some drown it out with drugs.

Others drink it away.

Some of us end up on street corners in conversation with the Void or in hospitals with padded walls staring directly into it, lost in chaos.

I turned the white noise machine on and closed my eyes.

"Jim," the voice said, "You there?"

But no one was listening.

About the Author

Dan MacDonald is a radio personality in Windsor, Ontario and Detroit, Michigan. He's active in community theatre, and is a collector of vinyl records.

IF YOU LIKED THIS BOOK, TRY...

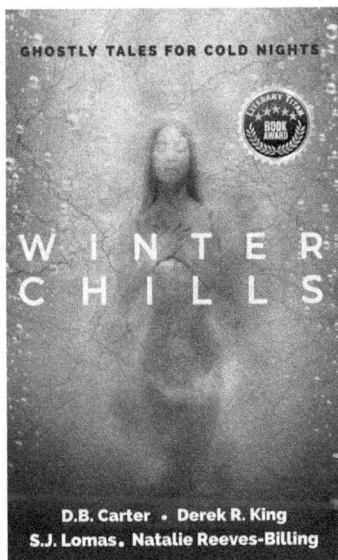

In the spirit of seasonal ghost stories, this wintry collection will send a tingle down your spine, but may also warm your heart.

Six short stories range from waiting for a mysterious midnight train, attending a party with an unexpected guest, a life-changing reunion for a miserable family, receiving a holiday greeting unlike any other, a visit from an unusual group of carolers, and a journey through a blizzard with a twist.

Grab a blanket, your favorite hot drink, and settle in for some Winter Chills.

Stories included:

By D.B. Carter: Departures and Arrivals

The Christmas Card

By Derek R. King: Defying Convention

By S.J. Lomas: The Holiday Party

The Carolers

By Natalie Reeves-Billing: Go With the Wind

Printed in the USA
CPSIA information can be obtained
at www.ICGtesting.com
CBHW031116231023
1466CB00001B/43

9 798987 977415